Texas Manhunt

Texas
Manhunt

Jackson Cole

THORNDIKE
CHIVERS

This Large Print edition is published by Thorndike Press®, Waterville, Maine USA and by BBC Audiobooks, Ltd, Bath, England.

Published in 2005 in the U.S. by arrangement with Golden West Literary Agency.

Published in 2005 in the U.K. by arrangement with Golden West Literary Agency.

U.S. Hardcover 0-7862-7593-6 (Western)
U.K. Hardcover 1-4056-3388-3 (Chivers Large Print)
U.K. Softcover 1-4056-3389-1 (Camden Large Print)

The text of this Large Print edition is unabridged.
Other aspects of the book may vary from the original edition.

Set in 16 pt. Plantin by Liana M. Walker.

Printed in the United States on permanent paper.

British Library Cataloguing-in-Publication Data available

Library of Congress Cataloging-in-Publication Data

Cole, Jackson.
    Texas manhunt / by Jackson Cole.
      p. cm. — (Thorndike Press large print Westerns)
    ISBN 0-7862-7593-6 (lg. print : hc : alk. paper)
    1. Hatfield, Jim (Fictitious character) — Fiction. 2. Texas Rangers — Fiction. 3. Texas — Fiction. 4. Large type books. I. Title. II. Thorndike Press large print Western series.
PS3505.O2685T494 2005
813'.54—dc22   2005002901

Texas Manhunt

1

Robert Morales stood at the end of the bar toying with a half-filled glass. Just over his head and a little behind him was a big hanging lamp, the wick turned high. Morales sipped from the glass occasionally, which a hovering bartender made sure was immediately refilled when empty, but his glittering black eyes never left the swinging doors some ten paces from where he stood. And his right hand hung limp by his side and close to the black butt of the heavy gun that swung low against his thigh.

A salty bunch frequented the Last Chance Saloon, many of them of dubious reputation. Half the men in there knew who he was, but because they also knew *what* he was, they did not speak to him.

Robert Morales was not one to invite casual conversation.

The air was charged with tension. The orchestra played offkey, the dance floor was deserted. At the poker tables players absentmindedly called three of a kind on a busted flush. Several oldtimers at the bar made the mistake of drinking water instead of whiskey. Men yearned to get out of there. Something was going to happen — they weren't sure just what. Whatever it was they wanted no part of it. But with Robert Morales' bleak gaze fixed on it, they didn't care to walk through that door. There was no telling how the outlaw might interpret such a move, and Morales was a killer devoid of fear or mercy. A man who considered himself the victim of bitter wrong, he was absolutely ruthless, unbelievably daring, and he had what often doesn't go with a fast gun hand — a cold, clear brain that could size up and evaluate a situation in a flash. He was utterly unpredictable and his reactions, mental and physical, were hair-trigger. Among other crimes, he had killed a sheriff, several deputies and a Texas Ranger. He entertained an implacable hatred for all things symbolizing law and order, and to him peace officers were vermin to be stamped on.

Robert Morales had no friends and no associates, and wanted none. Which was one important reason why his long and evil career had flourished in two countries and several states. There was no tracking down Morales through an intermediary. He rode alone. Out of the nowhere he came, and into the nowhere he vanished, leaving violence and death behind him.

He was tall, lean, sinewy. His flashing black eyes and his swarthy cheek bespoke his heritage of Spanish blood; but his hair, in singular contrast, was golden and inclined to curl. That mane of yellow hair was a brand mark of Morales. The Mexicans called him *El Dorado* — The Golden Man. But the sheriff who went looking for an outlaw with lean, smooth cheeks, a long cleft chin and golden hair might find himself taking his last look into the muzzle of a gun held by a man with jet-black hair and a black beard. Morales was an artist at changing his appearance.

The old bartender had known Morales a long time, had known him when he was just a reckless young cowhand who gambled and drank and danced with the girls like any other puncher. He drew close to the outlaw, busily polishing a glass, and said in a low mutter, his lips not moving —

9

"Bob, Jim Hatfield rode into town about an hour ago. They say he's looking for you."

"I know it," replied Morales, without taking his eyes off the door.

"There's a door from the back room leading into a dark alley," the drink juggler suggested.

"I know it," Morales repeated, still gazing at the swinging doors.

The bartender drew back with an almost imperceptible shrug. He had done all he could. He had liked Bob Morales in his younger days, and had known and liked his father before him. Bad as Morales now was, he didn't want to see him killed, and he figured, the way things were shaping up, that Morales had a very little while to live.

The slow moments dragged past, and Morales stood there, his unwinking eyes fixed on the door, while the tension grew unbearable and men clenched their sweating hands and tried to moisten dry lips with equally dry tongues. Anything would be better than this cold, deadly waiting. Even Morales' famous, *"Buenos noches, Senor!"* the sardonic, "Good night, Sir!" which were the last words his victim heard spoken on this earth. It was almost with relief that the occupants of the room saw the doors swing open and a man walk through.

He was a very tall man, broad of shoulder, deep of chest. He had black hair, long, level eyes of a peculiar shade of green, a hawk nose and a lean, powerful jaw. On his broad chest was the silver star of the Texas Rangers. Encircling his lean waist were double cartridge belts, from the low-slung cut-out holsters of which protruded the black butts of heavy guns. For an instant he stood gazing with narrowed eyes at the outlaw at the far end of the bar. Then his deep voice rang out —

"Robert Morales, in the name of the State of Texas —"

His right hand moved like the blurring flicker of a rattlesnake's deadly stroke. Morales' hand moved also. The two guns boomed together. Back and forth through the swirling smoke spurted the red flashes as the hanging lamp behind Morales jumped and flickered to the thunder of the reports.

Morales' hat turned sideways on his head. A lock of golden hair leaped from just above his left temple; but he stood firm and erect, peering through the smoke, as the tall form of Jim Hatfield crumpled forward and crashed to the floor to lie mo-

11

tionless, blood visoring his face with scarlet.

For a moment there was a deathly silence, while the smoke wreaths eddied upward. Then a voice spoke in hoarse, gasping tones —

"Good God! He shaded the Lone Wolf!"

Robert Morales laughed, a high-pitched, jeering laugh. His glittering eyes swept the silent room. He holstered his gun and walked to the door with long, lithe strides. He paused to gaze down at Hatfield's still form.

"Buenos noches, Senor," he said, and was gone into the night.

Instantly the room burst into turmoil. Everybody seemed to be yelling at once. The screams of the dance floor girls high-noted the uproar. The bartender jumped over the bar and ran to where Hatfield lay. He squatted down, thrust a hand inside his shirt.

"Ain't dead," he announced. "Heart's still going. Mighty slow like, though, and it looks like the whole top of his head is blown off. Somebody hustle out and get the doctor."

"What about Morales?" asked an excited cowboy. "Ain't somebody going to get *him?*"

"Anybody that wants Morales can go right ahead and get him," the bartender replied grimly. There were no volunteers.

The doctor arrived in five minutes, a white-bearded old border man who had been patching up gunshot wounds for fifty years. He made a swift examination.

"Slug hit high," he grunted in answer to the questions fired at him. "Is he going to die? How the Sam Hill do I know whether he's going to die? Doesn't appear to be any fracture, but I've a notion there's a bad concussion. Chances are he'll be up and around in a week, though. His sort is hard to kill. You say he didn't nick Morales? Wouldn't have believed there was a man in Texas who could shade him on the draw. Well, there never was a horse that couldn't be rode, and there never was a man who couldn't be throwed. Guess that goes for the Lone Wolf, too. All right, get a shutter, or a table top, some of you fellers, and pack him over to my office. I'll do what I can. Wait till I tie a bandage around his head. Oh, he can be moved, all right. If that slug didn't kill him, nothing will. And somebody telegraph the sheriff and Ranger Post Headquarters. Captain Bill McDowell will paw sod for fair when he hears about this."

Old Doc Beard was unduly optimistic. Three weeks went by before Jim Hatfield, his face haggard, his head still swathed in bandages, sat in Captain Bill McDowell's office at the Ranger Post and talked with the old Border Battalion commander.

"Jim," Captain Bill asked curiously, "did Morales really shade you on the draw?"

"Cap," Hatfield replied, "I don't know. He was fast, devilishly fast. But he did better than shade me — he outsmarted me."

"How's that?" McDowell asked.

"He's got the kind of a mind that takes in everything," Hatfield replied. "He never misses a bet. He knew I was looking for him, of course, and he didn't choose to trail his rope. He planned things so that the advantage of position would all be on his side. He was standing at the far end of the bar when I entered that saloon, waiting for me. He'd evidently made sure I'd learn he was there. Right over his head, just a little behind it, was a big hanging lamp swung so low that the bowl almost touched the crown of his hat. When I looked toward him the glare of that lamp hit me squarely in the eyes. About all I could make out was the outline of his shape, sort of like a shadow. I had a notion right then that I was going to get it. But there was nothing I could do. I had to play the hand. And Morales had the deck stacked in his favor. He may have pulled trigger first, I don't know, but I did pull trigger three times before I went down. I think he fired only twice, unless he shot again as I was going down, and I doubt if he did. I felt the wind of his first slug, then the sky fell on me."

"I see," Captain Bill said thoughtfully. "And he got clean away."

"Naturally," Hatfield answered. "I reckon everybody there was glad to see him go. He made a clean getaway and just vanished from sight, as he always does. He never works with a bunch and, so far as anybody seems to know, he has no associates. Which, of course, is in his favor."

"Another thing in his favor is the fact that you're a peace officer," the Ranger Captain growled. "As an officer of the law, you had to announce yourself and your intentions before reaching. That gave him an undue advantage, but a peace officer can't do it any other way. If it had been man to man, I'm willing to bet the results would have been different."

"Maybe," Hatfield agreed with a smile.

15

"Never can tell. Things work out funny sometimes."

"In one way he didn't get the breaks this time, though," Captain Bill mused.

"No?"

"No, he didn't kill you."

"That's right, he didn't," Hatfield agreed. As the Lone Wolf spoke, his eyes seemed to subtly change color until they were an icy gray, and his face set in grim lines. And Captain Bill knew that although the world is a big place, it wasn't big enough any more to hold both Robert Morales and Jim Hatfield.

"While I was busy getting well in Doc's place, I learned a little about Morales," Hatfield pursued reflectively. "The old bartender in that saloon knew him when he was younger, before he got started on the owlhoot trail. Seems his grandfather, a real Mexican *hidalgo,* came to Texas and acquired a good ranch and married a Texas girl. When he died the place de- scended to his oldest son, John Morales, who, incidentally, also married a girl from Texas. 'Pears John Morales, Robert's fa- ther, wasn't much of a cattleman, nor much of a businessman, either. A couple of smoothies flim-flammed him out of his spread and he died of a broken heart because of it. Then, a little after his father died, young Bob Morales walked into a saloon where the two schemers were playing cards, remarked, *'Buenos noches, Senores!'* and shot them both. Then he trailed his rope and went to the bad generally. Drifted down into Mexico and raised the devil and shoved a chunk under a corner there. Went to New Mexico and then to Arizona, leaving a trail of blood behind him. In Arizona, the Arizona Rangers got after him. Three of them trailed him to what they supposed was his hidden hangout and figured they had him hogtied. They didn't. Morales came up behind them, called his *'Buenos noches,'* and killed all three. Then he dropped out of sight for a while."

"To show up a few months back in Texas," Captain Bill interpolated.

"That's right," Hatfield nodded. "And killed Ranger Tom Wilson, in addition to robbing a couple of banks and running off a few herds, single-handed. I figure he's just about the saltiest and smartest outlaw Texas has ever gone up against. As reckless as Sam Bass, as vicious as John Wesley Hardin, as deadly as Kingfisher or Ben Thompson, and with more brains than all of them put together."

"Quite a gent all around," said Captain

Bill. "What else did you learn?"

"I learned that after Morales killed those two tinhorns, the courts investigated the whole matter and decided that the pair had really robbed John Morales of his property and that the spread should go to John Morales' next of kin. That, of course, was young Bob. But naturally the court ruled him out. The only one left, it seems, was a girl, the daughter of John Morales' brother, old Don Roberto's younger son, who went east and worked in a bank. He died and the girl came back to live with her Uncle John. I judged that Bob Morales liked her and she liked him. Well, the court ruled that the girl should get the spread. Best as I learn she has handled it well. And I learned something else, something liable to be mighty important. I think the bartender let it slip unintentionally — he seemed to have a bit of a soft spot for Robert Morales. 'Pears Morales has been seen in the neighborhood of that ranch a few times since he came back to Texas. Perhaps he has a real interest in the girl, or perhaps some other reason for hanging around there. So you see that gives me a line on Morales. I figure I'll be in shape to ride in another week or so and I aim to amble over in that direction. Not far from the town of Preston. There are silver mines around Preston, in addition to good range country, and I gather it's considerable of a pueblo. I've a notion I can drop in there without attracting any attention. Must be a lot of chuck line riders and others passing in and out of the section. And if what I learned from the barkeep is a straight tip, I figure I should have a chance of dropping a loop on Senor Morales."

Captain Bill nodded. He mused for a moment on what he had heard. The beginning of Robert Morales' outlaw career bore a singular similarity to what Jim Hatfield probably just missed being, thanks to the shrewdness and persuasive powers of Bill McDowell. Like Morales, Jim Hatfield had suffered bitter wrong. Just after he graduated from engineering college, wideloopers killed his father, callously and in cold blood. Young Jim, seething with anger, was about to set out to run down his father's killers. But Captain Bill got hold of him in time and showed him that riding the vengeance trail on your own is mighty risky business and liable to end you up on the wrong side of the law. He had persuaded Hatfield to join the Rangers and go hunting his father's killers with the law behind him instead of against him. Captain

19

Bill promised that it would be Hatfield's first chore as a Ranger and hinted that after he finished the chore he was free to resign from the corps. Hatfield finished the chore, all right, bringing the killers to justice, but it took a long time and before it was finished, Jim Hatfield was, as Captain Bill doubtless figured he would be, a Ranger. He had never regretted his choice. He had kept up his studies and planned to be an engineer some time. His technical knowledge had served him well more than once in the course of his Ranger activities.

Hatfield stood up, towering over the old Captain, who was himself a stalwart six-footer. "Think I'll amble over to the stable and see how Goldy, my horse, is making out," he said. "Then I figure to eat and rest a while. I'm not quite myself yet."

"You take care of that head," growled Captain Bill. "Doc Beard told me that if the slug had gone an inch lower you wouldn't have had any brains left inside your head."

"If there was any to shoot out," Hatfield replied wryly, thinking of how Robert Morales had maneuvered him into a position where the odds were all against him. "Well, so long, see you tomorrow."

Captain Bill watched his tall form pass

from the office and tugged his mustache.

"This should be plumb interesting," he mused. "Wolf against wolf! The two deadliest men in the Southwest pitted against each other. Well, though he lost the first hand, my money's still on Jim Hatfield."

But Captain Bill would not have been so confident had he foreseen the cold daring and uncanny ingenuity of Robert Morales.

2

The reward notice loomed grim and forbidding on the center post of the Alhambra Saloon, Preston's biggest. Sheriff Tom Cobert had nailed it there with purposeful blows less than an hour before. Cobert was young, ambitious and newly elected to office. He meant business.

The majority of the cattle and mining town's male population was at work at the silver mines south and east of Preston. But about every able-bodied gent not out of town at the moment, and quite a number of cowhands from the neighboring ranches, and chance visitors, were in the Alhambra eyeing the notice and discussing it between drinks or hands of cards.

It was not the first time a notice had been posted for the gentleman in question.

They were scattered all over the Big Bend country and north to the New Mexico line, and in several other states. But this time the ante had been considerably boosted. Cowmen, banks and stage coach lines had chipped in to make the pot really worth while. The glaring black letters proclaimed the fact in unmistakable terms.

$5,000.00 REWARD
DEAD OR ALIVE
OFFERED FOR THE
PERSON OR THE
BODY OF
ROBERT MORALES

It was followed by a somewhat flamboyant description of the notorious outlaw and a long list of his misdeeds.

"Gents," remarked an old waddie who lounged against the bar, "gents, that is a plumb hefty passel of dinero."

"Uh-huh," another nodded agreement, "and collecting it is a plumb hefty chore, too."

"Feller, you chawed out plenty," said the first speaker. "The gent who collects will sure earn his pay."

"I'm sort of new in this section — just rode over from the Nueces country," remarked a man in rangeland clothes. "Who is this Morales feller, anyhow?"

"Plenty of folks opine he's the Devil," the old waddie replied grimly; "and I got a notion they ain't far wrong."

"Is he Mex? Name sort of sounds like it."

The old waddie shook his head. "Nope, Morales is Texas born," he explained. "His grandfather came from Mexico — real old Spanish stock — settled in Texas and married a Texas girl. Robert Morales was born here, and so was his mother. He's a Texan, all right, although some folks 'low he looks a mite like a Mexican, when he happens to be wearing black hair instead of yellow. And he talks Spanish considerable. Seems to have a liking for it."

" *'Buenos noches, Senor!'* " somebody remarked signficantly.

"Uh-huh," nodded the old waddie, "that's it. That's what he always says just before or just after he's cashed in a gent. *'Buenos noches, Senor!'* has got to be Morales' brand, so to say. That's what he said as he plugged that young Texas Ranger Wilson, who'd been sent over from the Post to rid the section of the pest. Morales rode into Rosario, where Wilson was, called him out of a building and drilled him dead center and rode out of town. The sheriff and a couple of deputies chased him. Morales holed up in a thicket and drygulched both deputies, dropped a loop around the sheriff's neck, hauled him out of his hull and drove a knife through him. Next night he widelooped a herd fifty miles to the east. He's a heller, all right. Rides into a town all plastered with reward notices for him, sets down and plays monte or faro and rides out again without anybody knowing it was him, unless he takes a notion to announce himself with *'Buenos noches, Senor!'* or something like that. Trying to run him down is like chasing a shadow across the prairie at sunset. Doesn't ever seem to look the same as when the last time he was seen. One time he's got black hair, the next time it's yellow. One day his skin is dark, the next time it's light. Got plenty of wrinkles on his horns. He's salty and plumb bad, and the fastest gunhand in the whole Southwest."

A big hulking cowboy with bristling red hair and truculent eyes had been listening to the conversation, between frequent downings of redeye. Now he gave a contemptuous snort and tossed off his glass like so much water.

25

"I calc'late a jigger like Morales has got a reputation a sight heftier than *he* is," he rumbled. "It don't take over much guts or over much speed to plug some feller when his back's turned. Me, I'd sure like a chance to cash in on those reward pesos. I figure I'd rake in the chips, too, if I met this here Morales when I was looking in his direction."

The oldtimer eyed him mildly. "Maybe so, son, maybe so," he admitted, "but I still feel it would be considerable of a chore."

The big cowboy appeared to be working himself into a rage. He hammered on the bar with a ham-like fist.

"Who the devil is Morales!" he bellowed. "Just a drygulching half-oiler sneaking around in the brush. All I ask is a chance to line sights with him."

He pawed his heavy Colt half out of the holster as he spoke, shoved it back, half drew it again. Men began edging away from him, glancing askance at one another. With his left hand he hauled clinking gold pieces from his pocket and slammed them on the bar.

"There's a hundred pesos I'd give for a chance to meet that damned Morales face to face!" he stormed.

Midway across the room a monte game

was in progress. The players, intent on their cards, apparently paid no attention to the wrangling at the bar. Suddenly, however, a tall, slender, broad-shouldered youngish looking man with a darkly handsome face and black eyes of a strange brilliance cashed in and rose to his feet. He glanced about, strode lithely to the bar, pausing directly in front of the red-haired cowboy. He looked him up and down with his glittering eyes.

"*Senor,*" he said pleasantly, "I will take that money." His hand darted out, swept the gold pieces from the bar and pocketed them.

The cowboy let loose a bawl of anger. "Why, you horn toad hellion!" he howled and pawed at his gun.

"*Buenos noches, Senor!*" rang a clear, mocking voice. There was the crash of a shot. The cowboy crumpled up and thudded to the floor.

Robert Morales went sideways to the door like a flash of light. Two black gun muzzles, one wisping smoke, took in the whole room with their lethal sweep. Before the stunned occupants of the room could make a move, Morales was out the door.

With bellows of wrath the crowd surged forward, then back even faster as gunfire roared and lead hissed over the swinging doors. Through the pandemonium of men taking cover behind posts and under tables sounded a clatter of swift hoofs. The crowd poured from the saloon just in time to see the mounted Morales vanish from sight in the belt of chaparral west of the town.

"After the sidewinder!" bawled a dozen voices. "Get the sheriff!"

There was a concerted rush to the hitchracks. The sheriff was already coming on the run. There followed a wild confusion of rearing horses and swearing men who sought to back the frightened broncs. By sheer bellowing the sheriff got something resembling order, and an understanding of what had happened. He turned red with rage and outswore everybody else.

"There he goes!" a man yelled, pointing to where the trail left the far edge of the chaparral belt and writhed up a steep slope toward a notch in the hills.

Up the slope a horseman was speeding, bending low in the saddle. He already had more than a mile start, and he had appreciably increased his lead when the posse thundered into the thicket, leaving a practically deserted town behind.

At top speed they tore through the thicket and charged up the long slope. The

28

fugitive had already disappeared in the notch.

"We'll drop a loop on the hellion," swore Sheriff Cobert. "He slipped this time. The nerve of him! Downing a man right under my reward notice!"

"Ain't the first time he's done something like that," reminded the oldtimer who had discussed Morales in the saloon.

"It'll be the last time, though," the sheriff predicted grimly.

The posse boomed into the shadowy notch, easing their blowing horses a trifle but still maintaining a fast pace.

"Keep your eyes skun," warned the sheriff. "No telling what that hellion might pull, especially if he's cornered. And there's lots of thick brush alongside the trail."

Two more miles flowed under the speeding irons of the horses. Now the trail was winding through the Paisona Hills, a crooked snake track hemmed in by bare, steep, unclimbable slopes. And on the soft surface of the trail, for it had rained the night before, the prints of a speeding horse showed plainly. The sheriff let out an exultant whoop.

"He's heading for Mexico, but we've got him!" he exclaimed. "That's Skull Canyon and there's fifteen miles of straight-up-and-down rock walls before it opens out onto Skull Desert to the south. He can't turn off and we'll ride him down before he makes the desert. Sift sand!" Another ten minutes of fast going and the oldtimer suddenly raised his hand. "I heard a horse neigh around that bend ahead!" he exclaimed.

The posse jolted to a walk. Men clutched their weapons, peering nervously toward the ominous bend. A jutting cliff cut off their sight at the point where the canyon curved.

"Easy!" cautioned the sheriff. "No telling what that hellion is liable to pull. Horse coming this way. Hold it!"

Sitting their horses, guns out and ready, the posse waited, listening to the loudening hoofbeats.

Around the bend cantered a magnificent golden sorrel horse with a black tail and a rippling mane. He was a good eighteen hands high and had great liquid, intelligent eyes.

The rider was as noteworthy as the splendid animal he bestrode. Very tall — much more than six feet — he was broad of shoulder, deep of chest. He had black hair, a hawk nose, a rather wide mouth, the

corners grin-quirked, a lean, powerful jaw and long black-lashed eyes of a peculiar shade of green.

"Hell!" snorted the oldtimer. "That ain't Morales. Big as two of him and looks saltier."

Jim Hatfield pulled to a halt and eyed the gun-bristling posse with mild interest, his gaze centering on the sheriff's badge.

"What's up?" he asked. "Looks like a feudin'."

The sheriff recovered himself. "Did you meet a feller going the other way, fast?" he asked.

Hatfield shook his head. "Haven't met anybody in the past fifteen miles," he replied.

The sheriff swore luridly. "But you had to," he persisted. "We trailed the horned toad into this crack and he couldn't have gone up the sides."

"Not unless he sprouted wings," Hatfield agreed, his eyes on the ground. "By the way, did any of you fellers ever do any tracking?"

The oldtimer snorted. "Reckon I was following tracks before you were born."

"Well," Hatfield remarked dryly, "you must have forgotten a heap about it since then."

"What the hell you mean?"

"I mean," Hatfield replied, gesturing to the surface of the trail, "that unless my eyes are going back on me, and I don't think they are, I'm willing to bet a hatful of pesos that nobody has ridden south on this trail for a week. Take a good look."

Both the sheriff and the oldtimer dropped from their saddles and scanned the ground carefully. The oldtimer straightened up.

"Feller's right, Tom," he said briefly, "but how the deuce he could see it from up there in his hull beats me. We were skalleyhooting so fast and looking ahead all the time and didn't notice the trail had petered out. Now what's the meaning of this?"

The sheriff said several things, none of which would have sounded good in church. "What's the meaning of it?" he demanded. "I'm blamed if I know. With my own eyes I saw that hellion ride into the notch, and I saw those tracks he left turn into this canyon. Where in hoot did he get to?"

"Might have doubled back and headed on west," somebody suggested.

"Come on, we'll go see," said the sheriff. "Come along with us, feller. What's your name?"

"Jim Jackson," Hatfield replied, which was true. His middle name had been given him as a memento of the famous Confederate general.

The sheriff whirled his horse. The posse thundered back the way it had come. Hatfield touched Goldy with his knee and the sorrel quickly drew abreast of the sheriff and the oldtimer.

They bulged out of the canyon and onto the main trail. Hatfield glanced keenly about. "Sheriff," he said, "nobody's headed west on this track this afternoon."

The oldtimer dismounted and scanned the ground west of the canyon mouth. "Feller's right again," he announced. "Now what's the answer?"

The sheriff swore in helpless exasperation. Hatfield had also unforked and was studying the wide-spaced prints supposed to have been left by the speeding Morales. He straightened up and eyed the sheriff curiously.

"What time was that feller supposed to have made these tracks?" he asked.

"Less than two hours ago, why?" grunted the sheriff.

"Well, he didn't," Hatfield remarked conclusively. "These prints were made some time last night along toward morning, I'd say, right after the rain stopped. Look at the scum down in the bottom of the indentation, left by drying water. The surface is smoothed over as wouldn't be the case with a print made today when the ground was comparatively dry. Look for yourself."

The sheriff did look, and so did the oldtimer. He repeated what he had said twice before. "Feller's right." He looked Hatfield up and down. "Jim, just what kind of eyes have you got, anyhow?" he asked.

Hatfield smiled slightly and did not directly reply. "Sheriff," he said, "would you mind telling me just who you're chasing and why?"

The sheriff told him, vividly and profanely. Hatfield nodded his head thoughtfully.

"Robert Morales," he repeated. "I've heard of him. A salty jigger with plenty of wrinkles on his horns. I'd say he holed up in the bush somewhere east of here and let you fellers bulge past. Then he came out and headed back east."

"But in the name of creation, why?" demanded the bewildered sheriff.

"Having heard a little about Morales' methods and how he works, I'd say he wanted to get you and your bunch out of town," Hatfield replied quietly. "Looks like he purposely made a trail headed west sometime late last night. Fact is, I'm pretty sure of it. You'll notice that headed east from the canyon mouth is another set of tracks, tracks made by a horse traveling at an easy pace, and I'm about certain they were made by the same set of irons that made the others. My opinion is that he rode up this trail mighty fast, under cover of darkness, then turned his bronc and rode back to town. 'Pears he made sure you'd see him riding up this way hell-bent-for-election this afternoon. After he got into the notch you spoke of, he was out of sight, wasn't he?"

"That's right," growled the sheriff. Hatfield nodded again.

"Yes," he repeated, "it looks very much to me like the gent in question was anxious to get you and your posse out of town, for some reason of his own, doubtless a bad one. Reckon you just about cleaned the pueblo of able-bodied men when you rode out?"

"That's right," the sheriff agreed, looking startled and decidedly worried. "Nobody much left but a few storekeepers and bartenders."

"And perhaps some bank clerks," Hatfield added dryly. "Suppose you've got a bank in town?"

"We have, or did have," snapped the sheriff. "Feller, I believe you've hit it right, though how you figured it, I don't know."

"Anyhow," Hatfield remarked as he forked Goldy, "if I was you I'd hightail back to town just in case somebody might be asking for you."

The sheriff's reply smelled of sulphur. "Come on," he concluded, "we're heading for town."

The oldtimer, who appeared to be a person of precise words, said, "I've a plumb notion there isn't much sense in hurrying. If something happened in town, it's done happened some time ago."

3

Considerable had happened in Preston during the sheriff's absence. Three minutes after the posse disappeared up the notch, Robert Morales rode blithely from the thicket in which he had concealed himself and headed back to the town. He had assumed a disguise that was utterly simple but highly ingenious. He had merely changed his dark gray shirt for one of flaming yellow, knowing that the staring color would catch the eye of any chance observer and distract his attention from the wearer's face, against the assumption that said observer might have gotten a good look at Morales when he was in town before.

Preston had a decidedly deserted appearance when Morales rode down the main street. A face or two at shop windows glanced at the horseman and paid him no mind. Cowhands riding into town were of too common occurrence to excite curiosity or comment.

A one-story false-front housed the Preston bank, which did plenty of business due to the extensive mining and ranching operations of the section. The cashier and three clerks were busy at work when Morales walked into the bank. Before they knew what it was all about they found themselves staring into the business ends of two six-shooters.

The cashier made the mistake of reaching under the counter. He died, with Morales' bullet laced through his heart. Morales kicked in the partition door, herded the terrified clerks into the vault and made them stand facing the back wall with their hands raised. He leisurely filled a canvas sack with large bills lying ready to hand. Then he walked out and slammed the vault door shut. He paused to clean the cages and left the bank.

A man who had heard the shot came running down the street, a rifle in his hand. He died in the gutter. Another citizen peering through a window was showered with broken glass as a bullet shattered the window scant inches above his head.

Robert Morales mounted his horse and rode out of town, headed east. The Preston bank had been thoroughly cleaned out.

Three hours elapsed before Sheriff Cobert and his posse put in an appearance to find two dead men and a looted bank.

"A very nice plant," Jim Hatfield remarked to the raving sheriff. "Morales evidently deliberately kicked up a ruckus here in order to get you to chase him on the west trail. Then, knowing everybody who counted was out of town, he rode back and attended to business. Typical of him, from all reports."

"If I can just line sights with the sidewinder!" stormed the sheriff.

Hatfield nodded sympathetically. "Know where I can put up my horse for the night?" he asked.

"I'll show you a stable around the corner," the sheriff replied. "You can get a room in this building here, over the Alhambra. Good beds. Figure to coil your twine in this section for a while?"

"Sort of depends," Hatfield replied. "Looks like a nice section, but a feller can't eat regular if he doesn't work."

The oldtimer, who was standing on the other side of the sheriff, spoke up.

"Reckon there ain't no trouble about

that, son," he observed. "I've sort of took to you and there's a chore of riding over to my place if you care to hang your rain-shed in my bunkhouse. I'm Cale Jennings and I own the Swinging J over to the northeast of town."

"Biggest and best spread in the section," the sheriff put in. "You'd do well to ride for Cale."

"Doesn't sound bad," Hatfield tentatively accepted the proffered job. He liked the old fellow's looks. Jennings dressed like, and had the general appearance of, a down-at-heel cowhand, but this was not unusual for prosperous ranch owners who started out as waddies and were not overly changed by affluence. And the job would give him an excuse for hanging around in the section. He had never worked in the locality before and felt he had a pretty good chance of concealing his Ranger connections for a while. As a cowhand he might well gather information from sources that would be closed to an acknowledged peace officer.

"Suppose we go in and eat on it while you're making up your mind," suggested Jennings. "Chasin' owlhoots and not catchin' 'em makes me hungry. Be seeing you, Tom, I enjoyed the ride."

"You go to blazes!" growled the sheriff and stalked off, his back stiff. Jennings chuckled as he watched him depart.

"Cobert has the makings of a good peace officer," he commented, "but he's young and takes himself a mite serious. Let's put our broncs in the stable before we eat. Reckon they can stand the nosebag, too." He started to stroke the sorrel's nose as he spoke, but Hatfield held back his hand.

"Old Goldy isn't much on letting strangers touch him," he warned. "I'll introduce you and it'll be all right. He's a good injun, Goldy."

The sorrel ducked his head as if he understood. And he offered no objection to Jennings' hand.

"And he's sure some horse," said the ranch owner. "Never saw a finer looking one."

"He'll do," Hatfield answered.

After making sure that the animals' wants were taker care of, they repaired to the Alhambra and took a table by a window, where it was cool. Jennings chuckled as he glanced out at the deepening darkness.

"Wouldn't be a bit surprised if Morales was standing outside the window listening to what's said about him," he said. "He does things like that. Well, I reckon when a man doesn't give a damn whether he lives or dies, he gets that way. I've a notion Bob Morales is plumb ready and willing to cash in any time so long as he can take a few along with him. He seems to hate everybody's guts."

"What set him off in the first place?" Hatfield asked, hoping to get some information that would fill in the cracks in the bartender's story of Morales.

"It's a long story, but I'll tell it short," Jennings replied as they waited for the food to arrive.

Jennings' story was an elaboration of the bartender's yarn. "Reckon that was the first time Morales said, *'Buenos noches, Senores!'* when he plugged those two sharpies," he commented. "Must have sort of tickled his fancy. Anyhow he held onto it and it's a sort of brand mark of his now.

"Just one good thing came out of the whole mess," he added after pausing to drink some coffee. "The girl, Mary Morales, turned out to be bang-up at the cow business. Reckon she inherited old Don Roberto's cattle sense. She does a prime job of running the spread, and she's a good neighbor. The Walking R, her holding, is just east of mine."

Hatfield's interest quickened. Here was something worthwhile. He made a quick decision.

"Reckon I'll take that chore of riding you offered, sir," he said.

"Good!" exclaimed Jennings. "I was hoping you would. And now, if you've finished eating and it's okay with you, we might as well ride out to my place — it isn't far. Reckon our cayuses have finished eating too, by now."

"Funny somebody didn't recognize Morales in the saloon today," Hatfield observed as they walked to the stable.

"Not so strange," Jennings replied. "Been quite a few years since he was in Preston, although I've heard some folks claim they saw him in the section. And he's mighty good at disguises. His hair is naturally yellow, and he's not more than average dark. But with it dyed black and some stain on his face, like today, he looks like just another young Mexican riding up from below the Line. And who in blazes would expect the hellion to have the nerve and impudence to show up in Preston and pull what he did today? He's done things like that before, though. Acts sort of like he shoots — fast as greased lightning and dead center."

They saddled their horses and rode out of town, heading east by slightly north.

"My holdings run way over west and to the north, but my *casa* is close to my east line. More spreads up north and over west. Down there —" he gestured toward the rugged hills looming darkly against the southern sky — "is regular hole-in-the-wall country. An army could hide out there. And Mexico isn't far off. Made to order for a jigger like Bob Morales who knows every foot of the ground. If he didn't have to come out now and then for supplies, he could lay snug there forever."

Two hours of riding brought them to the Swinging J ranchhouse, a big white building admirably located in a grove of burr oaks.

"You sleep in the house tonight," Jennings directed. "There's a spare room. My range boss and some of the older hands squat in the *casa* with me. I like company and it's sort of lonesome in this big shack since my wife passed on a few years back. First let's comb the kitchen a mite and round up some cold chuck and steaming coffee. As I said before, mixin' with owlhoots always makes me hungry."

Later, Hatfield sat down on the comfortable bed in the room Jennings assigned him and thought the situation over. It was beginning to look like things might be working out to give him a much-needed break. He wondered why Morales had circled around back to the section where he started out. He must know he was taking a big chance, with folks liable to recognize him no matter how good he was at disguises. Hatfield figured he must have some definite reason for coming back to his original stamping grounds.

"Wonder if there's somebody hereabouts he's got it in for proper?" he mused. "Could be. He's sort of on the prod against everybody, it would seem. That happens sometimes when a man busts up his own life. Morales doubtless felt he was justified in those first two killings, though they were sort of snake-blooded. Being started on the run because of what he didn't consider wrong may have worked on his mind. He may have come back just to sort of even up with the section. That's one angle to keep in mind. But there's another angle, and it may be an important one. Most owlhoots have some sort of weakness that sooner or later causes them to get their comeuppance — cards, whiskey, women. It's the woman angle that's got me interested. Seems Morales thought pretty well of his cousin, Mary Morales, who now owns the Walking R, and she of him. That may be what brought him back. And that opens up another angle to consider. As Jennings said, a man might hide out in these hills forever and be safe, if he didn't have to leave his hole-up to get supplies. When a wanted man goes into a store, he's taking a chance. Somebody may recognize him and have an itch for reward money. But if there's someplace where he can slide in at night, load up a supply of what he needs and slide out again without anybody being the wiser, then he's sitting pretty. That could be it. Mary Morales and the Walking R ranchhouse may be his ace in the hole. Which gives me a notion."

He undressed, blew out the lamp and went to sleep.

4

The following morning Jennings took his new hand on a tour of the Swinging J to acquaint him with the range. Late in the afternoon they skirted the base of low but craggy hills that formed the Swinging J's eastern boundary.

"Just the other side of those rocks," remarked Jennings, jerking his thumb toward the rises, "is the Walking R holdings that Mary Morales runs."

Hatfield nodded, his eyes interested. He took careful note of the terrain.

The Swinging J hands proved to be a good bunch, mostly on the elderly side. Some of them had been with Jennings for nearly thirty years. The range boss, Jesse Mosman, was a grizzled oldtimer with twinkling brown eyes and a sense of

47

humor. He had ridden with Jennings during the turbulent days of their youth. He looked Hatfield over carefully and assigned him top-hand duties without hesitation.

"You look pretty husky," he told him, "so I'll just hand you the chore of combing those cracks and draws over to the east. Good water back in the canyons, but around the criks and holes it's sort of boggy and there's always some fool cow critter getting mired down and needing to be hauled out."

Hatfield accepted the chore with pleasure, for it worked in well with a certain plan he had formed.

Cale Jennings evidently liked the company of the new hand. Several times in the week that followed he asked Hatfield to accompany him on his rides to town. The old rancher, while having but little formal education, was widely read and he enjoyed discussing subjects with Hatfield that were a closed book to his other hands.

"Jim," he said suddenly one day, "there's times I can't make you out. You're a funny feller, for a chuck line riding cowhand."

Hatfield smiled. "Perhaps, for a chuck line riding cowhand."

Jennings eyed him curiously for a moment but refrained from further comment.

The town of Preston was booming. There was a constant stream of strangers coming and going. Wandering cowhands, hard rock men seeking work in the mines, bearded prospectors from the hills and the desert, and others who might fit into any category, mostly dubious. And there was a corresponding rise in lawlessness which kept Sheriff Cobert in a continually bad temper.

"You can't tell who or what's here," he fumed. "With all this coming and going I can't keep proper tabs on anybody. For all I know, Robert Morales, in corduroys and muddy boots and wearing whiskers may be settin' at the next table."

Hatfield was inclined to agree with the sheriff. The conditions were ideal for the shrewd and daring outlaw. If Morales were really still hanging around the section, he might easily make trips to town with little fear of detection. And Hatfield had an uneasy premonition that he was liable to bust loose somewhere any day. It would be simple for him to size up opportunities for one of his bold and unexpected strokes.

Meanwhile, there was plenty to do on the east range of the Swinging J. Hatfield performed the chores with quiet efficiency and Mosman, the range boss, nodded approval and left him alone to handle matters as he saw best.

"Never saw anything to equal him," he told Jennings. "He's got more cow sense than a dozen ordinary hands. But Boss, there's something funny about that big jigger. He does everything right, but he gives the impression that his mind isn't on what he's doing. Sort of like the whole business was just a means to some end, whatever the hell that could be. Hope we don't wake up some morning and find the ranchhouse gone, and him with it."

"I don't think you need to worry, Jess," Jennings chuckled. "I'll bet my last peso on Jim being an honest man, but I'll agree with you that he's sort of out of the ordinary."

"I just can't get over the feeling that I've seen him somewhere before," Mosman observed musingly. "Seen him or heard something about a feller of his general description, and I don't figure there could be two in Texas like that."

"Yes, when they make his sort, they usually bust the mold," Jennings nodded thoughtfully. "Just like that sorrel horse of his. They're a pair to draw to, all right."

"But don't expect to get three of a kind," grunted Mosman. "That just ain't in the cards."

Three days later, Hatfield proceeded to put his plan into execution. He rode up the slopes of the eastern hills toward the Walking R holdings. Picking out routes that were possible for Goldy, he worked higher and higher among the crags and chimney rocks. Finally he reached the jagged and broken crest of the range and rode eastward slowly and carefully, his keen eyes probing thickets and stony outcroppings, noting all actions of birds on the wing and the movements of little creatures in the brush. The passage of little more than an hour found him sitting his horse just beyond the edge of a belt of dense chaparral growth. Directly in front, a sheer cliff dropped a good two hundred feet to a fang of stone at its base.

A huge black shadow enveloped man and horse for an instant. Great wings fanned Hatfield's face and he had a glimpse of cold eyes and a powerful, angrily snapping beak.

The long line of the cliff was a nesting place of vultures, and the big fierce birds evidently resented his presence. Several

51

more swept by. Below, on jutting ledges, were the nests with watchful, mother condors brooding over the eggs.

"Bad jiggers, those fellows," Hatfield told Goldy, "but don't worry. They won't tackle you. They don't bother anything of any size that's alive. A critter's gotta be helpless before they go for him."

Ignoring the irritated vultures, he gazed eastward across the rolling rangeland. His eyes fixed on a large ranchhouse some two miles distant.

"Must be the Walking R *casa*," he mused. "Say, this is a regular lookout post. Couldn't be better. Easy to spot anybody riding to the house, even at night if the moon's bright. Feller, I've a hunch we'll spend some time up here."

He speculated about the ranchhouse and its surrounding buildings with interest, noting that a trail ran past the yard and forked just a little to the south, one branch evidently heading toward the broken hill country that flanked the desert and continued to the Rio Grande. For the moment he was oblivious to his immediate surroundings.

Something swished snakily from the growth behind him. Before he could turn or make a move a spread loop dropped over his head and shoulders and was instantly jerked tight, pinning his arms to his body just below the elbow joints. As he tried to writhe around, he was jerked from the hull to hit the ground with stunning force. There was a crackling in the brush, a pounding of fast hoofs and he was hauled along the ground as the taut rope swerved around a shallow arc.

Over and over he rolled, stones battering him, low bushes raking his face with stinging twigs. Over and over, closer and closer to the cliff edge and the yawning depths beneath. Another moment and his struggling body cleared the stony lip and plunged downward, bringing up with a jerk that drove the breath from his lungs and almost cut his arms in two. He thudded against the cliff wall and dangled half unconscious for an instant, just below the top of the cliff.

Then the rope swiftly paid out, ceasing with another jolting jerk. Raging and helpless, Hatfield swung back and forth, rasping against the stone, a good twenty feet below the jutting lip of the cliff.

There was a sound above. Hatfield craned his neck back and gazed up into a dark, regular featured face that bent over the edge. Black eyes of a strange and al-

most maniacal brilliance stared into his.
Thin lips writhed back from white teeth in
a veritable wolf snarl. Then a voice rang
out, clear and mocking —

"Buenos noches, Senor!"

5

Wordless, Hatfield stared up into the glittering eyes of the man above. The silvery voice rang out again —

"So! The famous Jim Hatfield! Roped and hogtied like a dumb yearling! So you thought to put one over on Robert Morales, eh? Last time you got a break. The bullet glanced off your thick skull, I suppose. You won't get one this time. And you won't horn in on my affairs again. This is my range, and I intend to hold it till I've cleaned it and collected a few debts I've got coming to me. I could have plugged you easily while you were sitting there trying to spot me. But this will be better. Better and slower. People say the bullet isn't run that can kill you. Maybe so, but I think I can count on the buzzards to do a proper chore. I'll just leave you swinging. And before they've finished, you'll be wishing for the quick mercy of a slug. Take a good look at me now, for you'll never see another face. They work on the eyes first, you know."

For another moment Morales stared down, his face contorted with hate. Then he lapsed into Spanish once more, a mocking farewell —

"Buenos noches, Senor!"

With his final sardonic, "Good night, Sir!" to his latest victim, Morales drew back his head and vanished from Hatfield's sight. A moment later he heard the beat of fast hoofs quickly fading into the distance.

Seething with anger that was directed chiefly at himself, Hatfield swung utterly helpless against the cliff face, with the black fangs of stone thrusting up nearly two hundred feet below.

"Morales was right!" he growled aloud, gritting his teeth against the pain of the rope cutting into his flesh. "Roped and hogtied like a dumb yearling! While I was trying to spot him, he was keeping tabs on me all the time. Pretty sure for certain he has been hanging about town in disguise. Of course he saw me and recognized me and, smart hellion that he is, figured I'd sooner or later come snooping around the Walking R ranch. Got me where he wanted me and tangled my twine for fair. Well, my hunch was a straight one. I've got that much satisfaction, anyhow. Came back to see that girl who's his cousin, I'd say. She may be working with him, or at least giving him a helping hand when he needs one. Uh-huh, I played a straight hunch, but it isn't likely to do me much good. Get out of here, you snake-eyed devil!"

His voice rose in a shout as one of the vultures swept past, almost touching his face with its wing-tips, snapping beak thrusting out.

The huge bird sheared off at the sound, then circled past again, though farther away.

"But it won't take the hellions long to figure they got me where they want me," Hatfield muttered. "They're vicious as sidewinders and have more brains. And they'll tackle anything that can't fight back."

For an instant, wild panic threatened to unnerve him. Then he got a grip on himself and considered his predicament from all angles.

It was hopeless enough. He could move his hands and lower his arms a little. But it was impossible for him to loosen the loop that pinned his upper arms to his sides. Try as he would he could not reach high enough. And the chances were, even if he could grasp the rope, not even his great strength would be sufficient to loosen it. He dropped his aching arms, gasping for breath, sweat pouring down his face.

The vultures were swooping close again, with glaring eyes and snapping beaks. Hatfield shouted and they sheered off, but not so far as at first. They were becoming bolder, convinced that the dangling thing against the cliff could do them no harm.

Another thought came to the Lone Wolf. He strained his right hand down, found that he could barely grasp the butt of his gun with his fingertips. With the greatest care he worked the butt upward. Another moment and he had a finger hooked inside the trigger guard. Then to draw the Colt from its holster was easy. He raised the weapon, straining the muzzle up and around. He found that he could line the barrel with the rope that pinned his arms. A slug would doubtless cut the twine. Then if he could manage to grasp the severed rope before he plunged to the rocks below, he could climb to the cliff top.

But there was a catch in the plan. Strain

as he would, he could not get the gun muzzle around quite far enough. He was practically sure to shoot himself when he pulled the trigger. His only chance would depend on how serious would be the resulting wound.

There was one thing left — the faint possibility that someone would hear a call for help. He felt he could fight off the vultures for a while yet.

He turned the muzzle of the gun outward and fired two evenly spaced shots, waited a moment and fired two more. It was the universally recognized rangeland signal that somebody was in trouble and crying for help. If anybody heard, he would investigate, and try to locate the source of the shots. He waited a moment and fired once more.

The vultures had swooped away with squawks of fright at the roar of the gun. Now they were wheeling and soaring some distance off. Hatfield was sure they would not return for some time. Setting his jaw against the torment of the rope eating into his flesh, he hung and waited, gripping the Colt with the last cartridge lined with the barrel, the cartridge he would use in a final desperate gamble against death by torture.

The minutes passed, slow, pain-fired

minutes. The vultures were edging nearer again, overcoming their fear. Hatfield gazed at the westing sun and estimated the time that elapsed. The pain in his arms was almost unbearable. He felt that anything would be a welcome relief from the flaming agony.

"If there was anybody within hearing distance they should be here by now," he muttered. "They couldn't very well miss finding me, with Goldy nosing around up there. Nope, there was nobody to hear. Might as well get it over with one way or another."

He raised the gun, inching the muzzle as far outward as possible and set it against the taut rope around his breast. Grimly he realized the angle was so sharp as to make a fatal wound almost certain.

But he had no choice. He set his teeth, pulled back the hammer to full cock. His finger tightened on the trigger.

Suddenly he heard a sound above. A voice called out, "Stop! what are you trying to do — kill yourself? Wait! Wait, I'll help you. I heard your shots."

Hatfield craned his neck and gazed upward. A girl's face was bending over the cliff. He could see her large, terrified blue eyes and her soft brown curls.

"Wait!" the girl called again. "I'll get a rope down to you and you can climb up."

Hatfield lowered his hand and let the gun slide back into its holster.

"I'll wait, Ma'am," he said, his voice hoarse with relief.

The face disappeared. A moment later a rope came dangling down the cliff. The girl leaned over, paying it out carefully.

"All right, get your foot in the loop, then I'll fasten it to a tree trunk," she called.

Hatfield managed to work one boot into the noose. "All right," he called back to her.

She vanished from his sight again. The noose tightened against the sole of his boot.

"It's fast," the girl cried. "Come on up."

But almost instantly Hatfield realized it was impossible. The rope that prisoned him had become tangled or twisted in the honda. He could not loosen the noose, and with his arms constricted, he could not climb the twine his hands were gripping.

"Can't make it," he called. "Can't get my hands loose."

There was a moment of silence. Then —

Before Hatfield could shout a protest she was over the lip of the cliff, small and slender, sliding down the rope. She could not pass his body, that was pressed against the rope. She rested one foot on his shoulder and, holding on with one hand, fumbled a knife from her pocket and opened it with her teeth. Then she leaned far down, set the edge against the taut cord gripping his body.

A moment of careful sawing and the rope parted, the noose fell away and Hatfield was free, his weight resting in the loop of the rope she had sent down to him. He gave a gasp of relief and began flexing his fingers to relieve the numbness of his arm muscles.

"Ma'am, you're a wonder!" he said. "Okay, climb back up and I'll follow you."

Obediently she began climbing the rope. She struggled upward a foot or two, slowly and awkwardly, and came to a halt, her feet dangling.

"I can't do it," she gasped. "I never tried to climb a rope before."

Here was a complication indeed. "Slide back where you were," he called. "Careful, now! For God's sake, careful!" He went rigid as one of her hands slipped from the rope and for an instant she dangled by the other. Then she got another grip and came down jerkily until her feet again rested on his shoulders.

"Take it easy now," Hatfield told her. "This is going to take some thinking out."

The vultures swooped near with snapping beaks. "Oh, those awful birds!" she exclaimed. "I believe they want to eat us!"

"Reckon they do," Hatfield agreed cheerfully, "but we'll fool 'em; they'll fly light-bellied this time. Ma'am, I believe I've got it. I can't climb up past you on this rope and the other one swung out of reach. Listen, and do just as I tell you. Slide down easy and get your arms around my neck, tight, and hang on. We'll go up together."

"You can never do it!" she declared, making no move to obey.

"Sure I can," he told her with a confidence he didn't feel. "It'll be easy. If I can't we'll go down together and give the buzzards a real good meal. Come on, now, do as I tell you. Don't worry, I'll support you with my free arm as you come down. Come ahead, now."

With a little sobbing moan, she began easing down the rope, slow inch by inch, till she could get her slender arms around his neck. Even under the circumstances, Hatfield couldn't help noticing the beauty of the piquant little face so close to his own.

"Ma'am, you're too darn distracting!" he chuckled as he got a good grip on the rope. "I'm plumb liable to forget what I'm trying to do."

He liked the spirit she showed when she answered, "When we hit the rocks down there you'll remember." He spared another chuckle and then saved his breath for what was to come.

Folks who had seen Jim Hatfield in action were wont to declare that there wasn't a stronger man in Texas; but here he had set himself a task that taxed even his mighty powers to the limit. He learned what an extra hundred pounds or so dangling from his neck could mean to a man clawing his way, slow foot by slow foot, up a jagged cliff by way of a smooth, seven-sixteenths hard twist manila strand. Fiery stabs of pain shot through his arms. Around his chest was an ever tightening iron band. His breath came in labored gasps, red flashes stormed before his eyes. The cliff top seemed a thousand miles away and constantly receding into the infinite distance. The shadows of the swooping vultures were as the icy flickerings of Death's cold wings. Each succeeding effort was a numbing agony.

The girl was suffering in sympathy with

his own travail. Little whimpers seeped past her red lips, her darkly blue eyes were wide as if in pain.

"If — if I let go, you can make it!" she gasped.

"Try it, and I bet I hit bottom before you do!" Hatfield panted grimly. "Shut up!" He slithered one bleeding hand upward and felt his knuckles graze against the projecting cliff lip. Another seemingly insurmountable obstacle to overcome.

But he made it! He got a grip on a jutting knob of stone and with a terrific effort that took the last vestiges of his ebbing strength, drew himself and his companion to safety. Utterly exhausted, he lay on the ground, gasping for breath to fill his tortured lungs, while strength flowed back into his tormented muscles. He glanced around and saw Goldy no great distance off and surveying with interest a small pinto that was evidently the girl's mount.

She was on her knees beside him, gazing down at him with wondering blue eyes.

"I wouldn't have believed it possible," she said. "I still don't know how you did it."

Hatfield's white teeth flashed in a smile. "And I wouldn't have believed it possible that there was anybody in the world like you," he declared.

The girl blushed prettily under his regard. Her red lips curved sweetly in an answering smile. But she instantly became grave again.

"Who in the world did such a thing to you, cowboy?" she asked.

Hatfield's face hardened. "Well," he said grimly, "as I recollect, the gent introduced himself as one Robert Morales."

The girl had recoiled sharply. One sun-golden hand raised and pressed against her lips. The color drained from her face till it was paper-white and her eyes seemed great purple pools of horror. For a moment she stared at him, then she got to her feet like one who is abruptly very old. She turned slowly and walked to her horse, swaying slightly, as if about to fall.

"I — I must go now," she said in lifeless tones.

Hatfield sprang to his feet. "But I haven't had a chance to thank you for what you did," he protested.

The girl lithely mounted her pony, settled her small boots in the stirrups. She gazed down at him.

"You don't need to thank me," she said. "I was glad to do what I did, and now I'm even gladder I had the chance to do it."

She started her horse forward, glanced back at the stupefied Ranger.

"You see," she said, just before she disappeared in the growth, "I am Mary Morales."

6

For long moments Hatfield stood staring at the bristle of growth. Finally he sat down on a convenient boulder and rolled a cigarette.

"Horse," he said to Goldy, "I know just how a man wading a shallow creek feels when he all of a sudden steps into a hole plumb over his head."

He smoked in silence for a few minutes, then resumed, while Goldy cocked his head and appeared to be listening.

"I should have tumbled first off to who she was. Guess I was a bit muddled. She's that sidewinder's cousin, the girl I figured he came back here to contact. Chances are she's in love with the horned toad, or at least has a soft spot for him because of the blood tie. And she saved my life and risked her own to do it. Sure puts me on an unpleasant spot after what she did for me."

He turned to contemplate the vultures that were swooping about with disappointed croaks, and their raucous cries served to emphasize what the blue-eyed girl's courage had saved him from. His face set in lines of pain, but his eyes were coldly gray as the granite cliffs. He rolled another cigarette and pondered the situation and how it might develop.

As he rode back to the ranchhouse, Hatfield did not discount the possibility that Morales might not immediately learn that he had escaped his trap. If so, he might possibly become less cautious and do something to tip his hand. For now Hatfield was convinced that the outlaw planned to stick around the section until he had consummated whatever vengeance was planned in his warped mind.

That Morales was close to if not wholly mad he was convinced. Insanity had glared in his eyes as he peered down from the cliff top. A madman with homicidal instincts, and with the uncanny cunning of the mad. Plus an utter disregard for personal danger. A nice combination to go up against, even for the Lone Wolf.

But Hatfield knew that more than his own life and reputation were at stake.

Morales had thrown down the gauntlet to the Rangers. He had callously killed one, and had come damn near killing another. Let one outlaw defy and outwit the Rangers and others would be inspired to try and do likewise. This Hatfield grimly vowed would not come to pass. Morales was ahead of the game so far, but Hatfield would never admit defeat till the last hand was played and Morales raked in the pot. Then it wouldn't matter much to him personally, for he wouldn't be around to see it done. It was life against life, with death as the forfeit for the loser.

He rode on into the scarlet and gold of the sunset. The leaves were tipped with amethyst and bronze and ripples of blue shadow rolled across the wide expanse of the grassland. The sad beauty of the twilight was in accord with his mood, one of weariness and depression which deepened even as the gloom between the tree trunks deepened until the spaces were like the black mouths of caves. The cheery lights of the Swinging J ranchhouse that turned the windows to squares and rectangles of pale amber were welcome to his eyes and with a sense of relief he got the rig off Goldy, saw that all his wants were cared for and then proceeded to the house.

He found old Cale Jennings just back from town and in a talkative mood. "Don't know what the section's coming to," complained Jennings. "Things that hadn't ought to, keep right on happening. This morning they found Judge Donavan dead in the trail just west of his *casa*. 'Pears his horse pitched him and busted his neck. Funny. Donavan was one of the best riders hereabouts, used to take all the contest prizes when he was younger. But I reckon nobody can ever be plumb sure. Donavan was a fine feller and a mighty good judge. Had a reputation for fair and wise decisions. Remember me telling you about how the Walking R spread was awarded to Mary Morales? Donavan was the judge who handled the case."

Hatfield suddenly looked interested. "Say they found him in the trail?" he asked.

"That's right," said Jennings. "Reckon he was heading for town. He usually rode in about that time."

Hatfield nodded thoughtfully. "Where'd they take his body?"

"Doc McChesney has got it in his office," replied Jennings. "He'll hold an inquest tomorrow. He's the coroner."

Hatfield nodded again, and did not

pursue the matter further.

But mid-morning of the next day found him in Preston, where he looked up the doctor's office.

McChesney proved to be a white-bearded old frontier doctor with keen blue eyes back of his spectacles. He nodded a cordial greeting.

"Come in, son," he said, "what can I do for you?"

Hatfield introduced himself. The doctor nodded his head vigorously.

"Well, well, so you're Cale Jennings' new hand, eh? He was talking about you yesterday. 'Pears to think mighty well of you. He was telling Sheriff Cobert he'd ought to make you a deputy in place of one of the terrapin-brained jugheads he has. Cobert opined it mightn't be a bad notion."

"Nice of them," smiled Hatfield.

Doc bobbed his head again. "What can I do for you?" he repeated.

"Doctor," Hatfield replied, "I'd like to have a look at Judge Donavan's body."

The doctor hesitated, but something in the steady gaze of the tall cowhand induced him to accede to the rather unusual request.

"Okay," he said. "Come on to the back room."

A moment later, Hatfield was gazing at

the corpse of a heavy-set, middle-aged man with a rather fleshy face. He studied the set features for several minutes, felt of the swollen neck with his sensitive fingers, and raised his eyes to the doctor's.

"Well," he said, "what do you think?"

McChesney parried the question with one of his own. "What do *you* think?" he asked.

"I think," Hatfield replied grimly, "that if you perform an autopsy you'll find the lungs congested."

McChesney nodded. "I'm something of the same opinion," he admitted.

"I'm no doctor," Hatfield observed, "but do *you* think that the abrupt fracture of a cervical vertebrae, such as would be occasioned by a fall, would induce visible traces of a certain amount of strangulation?"

"No," said the doctor, "I don't. I've been puzzling over it ever since they brought him in."

"And it is your opinion that his death was not caused by a fall from his horse?"

"I am not prepared to voice a definite opinion just yet," the doctor replied cautiously. "How'd you say he came to his death?"

"I'd say," Hatfield replied, "that his neck was broken by a man with long fingers and extremely powerful hands, broken by a wrenching twist, with a certain amount of choking necessarily preceding."

"No finger marks on his throat," McChesney pointed out.

"Right," Hatfield agreed. "That is what caused me to assume that the man in question has very long fingers. The tips of the fingers rested against the back of Donavan's neck. The man knew his power, and knew just where to apply the greatest pressure, which of course would be applied by the fingertips. I'd say he came up to Donavan, told him who he was and why he was going to kill him, and proceeded to do so in a way that apparently gave him the most satisfaction."

"But, good God!" exclaimed the doctor, "if you are right in your deduction, the man is a fiend!"

"He's all of that," Hatfield agreed grimly.

McChesney was eying him curiously. "Son," he said, "just who are you, anyway?"

"I told you my name," Hatfield smiled.

"Uh-huh, you told me your name, and you punch cows for Cale Jennings," the doctor said, "and you come in here, a chuck line riding cowhand, to all appearances, and display an unusual knowledge of anatomy and physical reactions. Fact is, I'm beginning to get a pretty good notion. And now I'm going to ask another question. Presuming you are right in what you just said, have you any idea who killed Judge Donavan?"

"I have," Hatfield replied quietly.

"So far as I know, Donavan didn't have an enemy in the world," the doctor said slowly. "He was noted for the fairness of his decisions, and many's the time he got litigants together and persuaded them to settle their differences amicably and be friends. Why should anyone want to kill him?"

"A man with a twisted mind, who nurses the illusion that he has suffered wrong sometimes reasons in strange ways," Hatfield said. "The man in question is convinced that Donavan did him a great injustice. Do you remember the matter of the Walking R ranch, which was handed over to Mary Morales?"

"Why, yes," replied the doctor.

"Then you should be able to guess who killed Judge Donavan," Hatfield said.

"You mean Robert Morales?"

"Can you think of anybody else?"

"No, I can't," admitted the doctor, "and the way you put it, it begins to sound logical."

"I've pretty good reason to know that Morales is out to get several people in this section," Hatfield said. "Do you know of anyone else against whom he might hold a grudge? They should be warned of their danger at once."

The doctor slowly shook his head. "Most everybody who had anything to do with that matter is either dead or has moved away from the section," he said.

Hatfield nodded, but he could not agree with what McChesney said. When he peered over the cliff top, Morales had clearly intimated that he had more than one act of vengeance to perpetrate. That he had killed the judge who turned over the Walking R to Mary Morales, Hatfield was convinced. But who else was the vindictive outlaw after? If he could just find out he might be able to save the other victim or victims.

The old doctor was pacing his office with nervous strides. "Son, what the hell am I going to do?" he asked. "I'm coroner, you know, and this afternoon I'm to hold an inquest. Shall I lay what you've told me before the jury? You'll have to admit that the whole thing will sound a bit fantastic to a cow country jury. Everybody is convinced that Donavan fell off his horse and busted his neck."

Hatfield rolled a cigarette and sat down to better consider the matter. He smoked a few minutes and reached a decision.

"If I were you I'd keep quiet about it," he said. "It would kick up an awful row and doubtless Morales would hear about it if he's still hanging around the section, which I think he is. It might cause him to move faster against whoever else he's got branded for a killing. The law wouldn't have much of a case against him in this instance, anyhow, and, which is more to the point, the law hasn't got Morales."

"My sentiments," agreed McChesney. "We'll just let things stand as they are and the jury can bring in whatever verdict it's of a mind to."

Hatfield nodded and rose to his feet. "Hope you won't consider me coming here as I did an intrusion," he said.

"I don't," the doctor answered shortly. "By the way, how is old Bill McDowell? I used to know him pretty well."

"Last I heard he was still up and kicking," Hatfield replied with a grin. He chuckled over the old doctor's canniness as he rode back to the spread. "Spotted me the minute I came in, I've a notion, but never once let on. Those old jiggers are smart, and hard to throw off balance. Well,

77

another count against *Senor* Morales, but who in blazes else is he twirling his loop for? If I can just find out in time, maybe I can prevent another killing."

7

Hatfield debated his next move. The upshot of the matter was that he spent three wearisome nights keeping close watch on the Walking R ranchhouse. And nothing happened. No furtive horseman rode out of the shadows to approach the ranchhouse that lay dark and silent and clearly outlined in the moonlight. Nobody left the building, no blurred shape moved on the wideflung rangeland that lay silvery soft with sleep. Coyotes yipped on the hilltops, owls voiced querulous plaint in reply, whippoorwills sounded their mournful calls. But only these homely sounds of nature broke the silence. Hatfield began to wonder if the killing of Judge Donavan wasn't the last "chore" Morales had in mind.

But he didn't think so. The outlaw had

hinted that he expected to make some more rich hauls before he trailed his rope out of the section. The question was, where would he strike? Hatfield hadn't the least notion, any more than he had any idea where to look for Robert Morales. And then, the evening of the day after his third fruitless vigil, he heard something that caused him to do some serious thinking. When he rode into the ranchhouse, his face haggard, his eyes red-rimmed from lack of sleep, he found old Cale cheerful and talkative.

"We want to figure to ride to town to-morrow night," he told Hatfield. "The pueblo will be lively. Tomorrow is payday for the Golconda Mines over to the west, and the miners will all be in for a bust. Payday for most of the spreads hereabouts, too. We figure to hit the same day as the mines. Gives the boys a chance for a mite of diversion when things are booming. Lots of money be spent in Preston to-morrow night. The stage that delivers the payroll dinero from the banks to the mines will be packing between thirty and forty thousand dollars."

"Would be a nice haul for somebody," Hatfield commented. "Stage ever been held up?"

"Not much chance of that happening with three guards and the driver all loaded for bear," Jennings replied. "It was tried a couple of times a few years back, but the gents who came looking for trouble got it handed to them till it ran out of their ears. Nope, the Preston stage don't have anything to worry about. Would take a mighty shrewd and salty hombre to put it over. Would be considerable of a chore."

"The sort that might appeal to a gent who likes to do things the hard way and outsmart real smart folks," Hatfield observed thoughtfully.

"Could be, but everything would be against him," said Jennings. "The trail runs along the base of the Vingaroon Hills almost the whole way from Preston to the mines. On one side the slopes are steep and the brush doesn't grow down to the trail. Sag water has wiped the lower hundred yards or so clean. On t'other side there's always a drop down into gulleys, sometimes as much as a hundred feet and never much less than twenty. No good hole-ups for an owlhoot with notions. He can't step out of the brush and say 'elevate!' He'd have to ride a ways without cover, and old Critch Muller, the driver, can dot the eye of a horned toad at thirty paces with his old Smith. And the guards are nigh as good with their Colts, to say nothing of sawed-off shotguns and rifles ready to hand. Nope, I figure only a mighty narrow-between-the-ears gent would even think of making a try for that payroll."

Hatfield went to bed a little later. "Want to get an early start over to the hills tomorrow," he explained, "seeing as we're headed for town tomorrow night."

Jennings agreed it was a good notion and turned in early himself.

Everybody was still asleep when Hatfield left the ranchhouse a little before dawn. He wanted to be in the Vingaroon Hills by sunrise, so that he'd have an opportunity to look over the lay of the land.

"Horse, I'm playing a hunch," he told Goldy. "May be a loco one, but we haven't gotten very far by acting sensible, so we'll just try something else for a change. Yes, it may sound loco, but somehow I've a feeling that a try for the mines' payroll would be just the sort of thing that would appeal to Morales. From all accounts, he's mighty good at doing things folks figure to be impossible. Like robbing the Preston bank, for instance."

The hills, so-called, proved to be a long,

low, irregular ridge a good fifteen miles in length. The road, built by the mining company, ran along its base. Jennings' description of the terrain proved to be pretty accurate. The lower slope was almost barren of vegetation, the scattered straggle of stingy growth providing no adequate concealment and never encroaching on the trail. Beyond the outer lip of the road were slopes that plunged steeply into water-scoured dry washes.

It would be possible for a horseman to ride the floor of the gulleys, Hatfield decided, but to think of a man, or half a dozen, for that matter, holding up the stage from the gulley floor was ridiculous. He wouldn't stand a chance. Apparently the only possible procedure was to meet the stage head on in the open trail. And with an armed driver and three vigilant guards ready for business, such an act would be tantamount to quick suicide.

"Plumb impossible, or so it would seem," Hatfield mused. "But Morales has proven he's at his best at doing what just naturally can't be done. If there's a possible way to lift that payroll, I'll bet my last peso he's figured it out. I never felt a stronger hunch, and I'm going to play it right up to the hilt."

He found that he could ride the crest of the ridge with the trail, a thousand yards or so beneath him, always in sight. In the shadow of a convenient tree, he pulled up, rolled a cigarette and made himself comfortable until the stage, which would leave Preston early, should put in an appearance. He could plainly see the smoke of the mining town, which was no great distance to the east. If Morales really had something in mind, it was highly unlikely that he would pull it close to town.

About two hours after sunrise the stage appeared, a bouncing dot in the distance that swiftly grew to a clumsy, lurching vehicle drawn by six mettlesome horses. There were two men on the high seat, the driver and one of the guards. The other two who were not in sight, Hatfield surmised were inside the stage with the doors locked. He gathered up the reins, waited till the coach was directly opposite where he sat his horse and a thousand yards or so below. He spoke to Goldy and the sorrel moved along in the shadow of the growth that fringed the crest.

For mile after mile Hatfield paced the stage, and nothing happened. The road, with frequent bends, stretched on into the distance, shimmering whitely in the sunshine, utterly deserted.

"Beginning to look like we're riding a cold trail, horse," he told Goldy. "Nobody in sight anywhere, unless he's down in that gulley under cover. And the only thing he could do from down there is to take a pot-shot at those jiggers on the seat, which wouldn't do him much good. Even if he managed to wing one, the pair inside would have all the advantage on their side. He'd never be able to climb up the sag from the gulch, and he'd be no better off if he did manage to make it to the trail. Yes, I'm afraid my hunch wasn't a straight one after all. Well, we've had a nice ride in the cool of the morning."

Nevertheless, he continued to pace the lurching vehicle, his keen eyes searching the terrain. But they were not quite keen enough to spot the highly ingenious trap laid for the Preston stage.

Old Critch Muller, the driver, pretty well occupied with keeping his six half-wild horses from climbing the trees, still found time to shoot searching glances up the slope ahead and into the gulley to his right. Old Critch was taking no chances, not with nearly forty thousand dollars in the strongbox inside the coach. There was no growth to speak of for a hundred yards or so up the slope on the left, but there were bristles on the floor of the gulley which here was better than thirty feet below the trail, the side of the sag steep and rocky, with a noticeable overhang where rushing water had scoured the sides of the coulee.

Hank Blivens, the outside guard, was also very much on the alert, sweeping the trail ahead with his gaze, ready sawed-off cradled across his knees. Inside the coach, Fred Cooley and Arch Simon smoked comfortably, peering out the windows from time to time. They couldn't see much but knew they would get ample warning from Muller and Blivens if anything untoward came into sight.

As the stage neared a sharper turn than usual, the vigilance of Muller and Blivens increased; but as they swung around the bend a straight stretch of nearly a half mile lay before them, silent, deserted. Both relaxed. Then Blivens let out a warning shout —

"Keep to the left, Critch, there's a rattlesnake coiled in the middle of the trail!"

Muller also saw the reptile. His grip tightened on the reins and he was about to swerve the leaders toward the upward slope when Blivens yelled a second warning —

"There's another one, a big one, coiled right up close to the bank. To the right,

Critch! to the right!"

Swearing under his breath, Muller jerked the reins in the opposite direction and swerved the snorting leaders until the coach wheels were grinding the very lip of the trail.

"Hey!" Blivens exclaimed suddenly, "that snake looks de—" His voice broke off in a startled yelp that was drowned by a rending crash. The unwieldy vehicle lurched wildly, careened sideways as the earth gave way under the outer wheels. An instant more and it toppled over the lip and went rolling and sliding to the gulley floor, the tangled horses screaming with pain and fear, the guards inside the body letting out howls of bewildered panic that abruptly ceased as the coach hit the gulley floor with a resounding crash.

Old Critch Muller, flung far out from his high seat, lay motionless on his back, arms widespread. Blivens, blood pouring down his face, was flopping and sprawling, trying to get to his hands and knees. Strangled croaks came from inside the coach as Cooley and Simon, bruised, battered, all their breath knocked out, tried to pump some air into their tortured lungs. And from a bristle of growth nearby rode a tall horseman, the sun glinting on his golden hair.

8

From the ridge crest, Hatfield saw the stage go off the trail. He hadn't the least idea what had happened, but he knew it wasn't in the books. He whirled Goldy and sent him charging down the brush grown slope. An instant later he saw the lone horseman riding toward the stage.

Hank Blivens, the outside guard, had struggled to his hands and knees, his head weaving and jerking as he made a mightly effort to gain his feet. From the horseman's side spurted a puff of whitish smoke. Before the thin crack of the shot reached Hatfield's ears, he saw the guard flatten out like a stepped-on frog and lie motionless.

"Robert Morales, sure as hell!" he exclaimed. "Trail, Goldy, trail!"

More smoke spurted. The outlaw was firing bullet after bullet into the overturned and shattered coach.

"Trying to do for the inside guards, the snake-blooded hellion!" Hatfield muttered as he slid his Winchester from the saddle boot. He clamped the butt of the long gun against his shoulder. The chances of scoring a hit at that distance, shooting downward from the back of a racing horse were negligible. But he could at least distract the outlaw's attention.

"And if he's got a rifle in his saddle boot, I'm a sitting duck!" he muttered grimly as he tried to line sights with Morales.

Which was true. He would be an easy target riding down the slope and would doubtless be dead long before he reached the trail. Face grim, he squeezed the trigger.

Morales jerked around as the slug whined past his head. Hatfield could see the glint of the sixgun in his hand. But he didn't raise the weapon, knowing that the range was too great for a Colt. And he didn't reach downward toward his thigh. Evidently he did not have a rifle.

"Trail, Goldy!" Hatfield shouted and pulled the trigger as fast as he could work the ejector lever.

For a moment Morales gazed cooly up the slope, with lead whistling all around him. Then he turned his horse and galloped down the gulch, swinging low and sideways in his saddle until he was almost hidden by his mount's neck. When Hatfield pulled his blowing, snorting horse to a halt on the trail, he was just passing out of sight around a bend a quarter of a mile distant. Pursuing him was out of the question, even if the smashed coach and its occupants hadn't required immediate attention.

"Anybody alive down there?" Hatfield shouted. A muffled cry answered his hail, and a sound of pounding inside the stage. Hatfield dismounted and slid down the bank to the floor of the gulch. A single glance told him that Blivens, the guard, was dead. Old Critch Muller, the driver, was groaning and thrashing about and apparently on the verge of regaining consciousness. Hatfield decided he would do for the moment. He hurried to the coach, which lay on its side. The horses had exhausted themselves with their struggles and lay moaning and sobbing but apparently not seriously injured.

"Be with you in a minute and cut you loose," Hatfield told them, and gave his attention to the coach. The door of the upper side had been jammed by the crash and although the guard inside was pounding on it he could not open it. Hatfield seized the handle, put forth all his strength and tore the door open. Out popped a wild-eyed, bloody face. From the shadowy interior came a sound of moaning and cursing.

"Feller," said the owner of the face, "I don't know who you are or where you came from, but I'm sure glad to see you!"

Despite the seriousness of the situation, Hatfield had to chuckle. The face bobbed down again. "Wait a minute," the voice said, "Arch Simon's down here with a hole through his shoulder. I'll boost him up and you haul him out."

A second face appeared, white and twisted with pain and sputtering curses. Hatfield got his hands under the man's armpits and with a mighty heave lifted him through the door and set him on his feet, weaving and cursing. The other guard climbed out unaided.

"It's high up through the top of the shoulder," panted Simon. "Hurts like hell and the shock made me sick, but I don't figure it's bad. Wait till I get my breath back. You all right, Cooley?"

"Fine as frog's hair 'cept for my skull busted open," answered the other guard, wagging his bloody head. "Good God! It looks like poor Blivens is done for."

"He is," Hatfield said. "And now can you tell me what the devil happened?"

"Darn if I know," said Cooley, "I heard Blivens yelling something about snakes, then the coach swerved over to the side of the trail and the next minute we were going down the sag, over and over. I hit my head against something and saw stars and comets, but it didn't knock me out. Then I heard a horse coming this way and a shot, the one that did for poor Blivens, I reckon. There was more shots and slugs commenced coming through the coach. We hunkered down low as we could, but the sidewinder was getting the range. Then all of a sudden he stopped shooting and we heard him ride away. Then we heard your beller and figured that help had come."

Hatfield nodded. "See what you can do for his shoulder while I take a look at the driver," he directed. "He 'pears to be coming out of it."

Old Critch was sitting up looking dazed and fingering a sizable lump on his forehead.

"Snakes," he said in answer to Hatfield's

question. "Snakes in the road. I pulled way over to miss 'em and down we went. What in Sam Hill made that bank cave in, I wonder?"

Hatfield walked over to the jumbled mess of earth and stone. He glanced up to the gap in the lip of the slope. His gaze centered on a splintered timber.

"Pretty clever," he said to Muller who had gotten to his feet and staggered over to join him. "Hollowed out the bank under the trail and propped it up with some slabs and spindly posts. When the weight of the stage came onto the spot, the earth gave way and down she went. Smart jigger, and not afraid to work. Must have taken him several nights to do the chore. He hollowed out more than thirty feet. See, there are some of the posts still standing."

Old Critch swore blasphemously. Hatfield scrambled up the bank to the trail. He quickly spotted the dead snakes carefully looped to simulate life.

"Simple and smart," he muttered. "Driver would naturally pull over to keep his horses from getting bitten. That hellion is a bunch all by himself. Well, I did a little better this time, though he gave me the slip. Maybe the luck's due for a change."

He slid back down the bank and joined

Muller and Cooley who were cutting the horses loose from the tangled harness. Simon, a handkerchief bound about his shoulder, was sitting with his back against a boulder and dragging on a cigarette. Hatfield decided his wound was not dangerous.

"Think you can ride bareback to town?" Hatfield asked him. "You should have a doctor look at that shoulder as soon as possible."

"I can make it," grunted Simon. "I'm feeling a sight better."

"Okay," Hatfield nodded. "We'll haul one of those cayuses up to the trail — they don't appear to be hurt aside from cuts and bruises — and you and I'll ride to town and notify the sheriff. You other fellows hole up here with your rifles. I don't think that sidewinder will come back, but best not to take any chances. He's smart as a treeful of owls and vicious as a Gila Monster."

"Tell 'em at the bank to send a wagon or something to pack this damn strongbox to the mines," said Muller. "Looks like the boys will get their pay on time after all, which it didn't look like a little bit ago. Son, if you're in town tonight, you won't stand a chance of not getting drunker'n a biled owl on free drinks. Much obliged again for everything. If you ever want somebody killed or a church burned down or something, don't wait a minute to call on us."

Sheriff Cobert was an outraged man as he listened to what Hatfield and Simon had to tell him.

"And are you sure it was Robert Morales?" he asked.

"Well, I didn't get close enough to him to make a positive identification but the gent in question had yellow hair and was of Morales' general build, from all accounts," Hatfield replied. "And if there is somebody else in this section capable of pulling such a chore, I'd hate to be sheriff of the county."

"I'm beginning to wish I'd stuck to punching cows," the sheriff said gloomily. "I'll send a wagon and a flock of deputies to escort that payroll to the mines, and another wagon to bring in poor Blivens' body. It was a fine chore you did, feller, a might fine chore. I only wish you'd got close enough to the skunk to ventilate him. You'd better walk over to the bank with me; they'll have some things to say to you. The bank would have had to stand the loss, you know."

"Some other time," Hatfield replied. "I've got to get back on the job. Liable to get fired as it is."

"If you do, I'll work over Cale Jennings till he looks like the American Flag!" Cobert promised.

Hatfield spent the remainder of the day on the Swinging J east range, hauling out a few bogged-down cows and checking the head of stock in some canyons. When he rode back to the ranchhouse, about sundown, he learned that Jennings had already gone to town.

"He told me to tell you that he'd meet you in the Alhambra," Mosman, the range boss, said. "Guess most all the boys will be there. It's their favorite hangout on big nights like tonight. I'll see you there later."

Hatfield ate a good supper and after a bath and a shave rode to town with some of the older hands. Things were already booming when they got there, with a promise of more to come. Hatfield quickly learned that he was a marked man. Several prominent citizens stopped to shake hands and congratulate him and Muller's prediction anent the free drinks had not been an exaggeration.

Cale Jennings eyed him curiously when they met in the Alhambra.

"Jim," he asked, "what the devil were you doing over in the Vingaroon Hills this morning? They're not Swinging J range."

"Just felt like taking a little ride," Hatfield smiled. "Hope you don't mind."

"If I said so and somebody heard me, I'd likely get lynched," Jennings replied. "You're just about the most popular man in this pueblo tonight. I just couldn't help but be a mite curious. But I'm not going to ask you any questions you don't feel like answering. I'm beginning to get a nice little notion all my own, anyhow. And any time you get a notion to take a ride somewhere, go right ahead and don't mind me."

Hatfield grinned and ordered a drink.

Jennings was justified in his promise of a lively evening. The crowds in the dusty main street steadily increased, constantly augmented by the arrival of cowhands from the more distant ranches. The bars were lined three deep, the roulette wheels were nigh onto burning out their bearings, the dance floor creaked to the pounding they were receiving. Dealers at the tables were constantly calling for new decks. Dice skipped across the green cloth like spotty-eyed devils. Song, or what passed for it, was beginning to bellow forth through open windows. Musicians scraped and strummed a quickened tempo. The air reeked with tobacco smoke and the tang of spilled whiskey soaking into the sawdust. Hatfield shrewdly suspected that before the night was over it would be supplemented by the pungent whiff of powder smoke and the raw and piercing smell of fresh blood. When the redeye, the gambling fever and the rivalry for the favors of women began getting in their licks, tempers would become frayed and trigger fingers would itch.

But such was to be expected in a turbulent frontier town where men were filled with the lust of life and had gold in their pockets that ached to be spent. There was a steady clink of bottle necks on glass rims, the solid plunk of gold pieces on the "mahogany," the soft slither of card on card and the monotonous drone of the dealers. Beneath the lanterns hung on poles that answered for street lights the thickening crowd eddied and swirled. The scene was vividly splashed with color as white shirts and blue shirts and shirts of red plaid vied with yellow neckerchiefs and scarlet mantillas. Mexican *Vaqueros* in black velvet adorned with much silver added a dark rich note. The short-skirted dress of a hurrying dance hall girl was like a flickering flame amid glowing coals.

The biggest and most boisterous crowd was in the Alhambra. Old Cale Jennings chuckled as he gazed on the colorful scene.

"Makes a feller feel sorry he's getting old," he said. "Oh, to be fifty again!"

"I've a notion from the looks of things that some gents hereabouts will never see fifty," Hatfield replied, a bit grimly.

Jennings nodded sober agreement. Already several incipient rows had been squelched by vigilant bartenders and floor men, but the tension was mounting and most anything was liable to bust loose at any time.

"And this diggin' is peaceful compared to some of those rumholes farther down the street," observed Jennings. "Funny how things work out, for no sensible reason so far as you can figure. There's always been a certain amount of friction between the cowhands and the mine workers — they don't see things eye to eye in lots of instances and they don't understand each other. Well, by some plumb loco brand of reasoning, the miners have decided that because Robert Morales was once a cowman, the cowmen of the section are to blame for that try for the mine payroll. Ever hear of anything so plumb weasel-brained?"

Hatfield looked grave. "It doesn't make sense," he admitted, "but I've heard of just such things causing a lot of trouble. It could happen here. I've noticed that the arguments that have tried to start in here tonight have been between mine workers and punchers."

Jennings nodded soberly. "I've told my boys to stick to themselves and not mix up with the miners," he said. "So far they seem to be obeying orders, but you never can tell."

Rolf Owens, who owned the Alhambra, strolled over for a word with the ranch owner.

"Rolf," Jennings said, "you're getting rich."

"Been taking in plenty, all right," Owens admitted. "I've emptied the tills and the banks three times already so far and stashed the dinero away in the safe in the back room. Should do pretty well if the hellions don't start a ruckus and bust up all the furniture. I reckon we can handle 'em, though. I got five extra floor men on the job tonight and they know their business."

"You're lucky in getting the steadiest of

the hands and the mine men," Jennings commented. "I recollect you having a wiring or two in here on paydays but never anything serious."

"Yes, it usually amounts to nothing worse than some punching and scuffling," Owens agreed. "Different farther down the street. Powder burned there sometimes. I'll send over a round of drinks. Enjoy yourselves, fellers."

The drinks arrived and Hatfield and Jennings conversed on various matters, mostly dealing with range work. Suddenly the ranch owner's eyes widened.

"Now what the blazes is *she* doing here on a night like this?" he exclaimed.

Following the direction of his gaze, Hatfield saw a girl who had just stepped through the swinging doors and was glancing around the room as if in search of somebody. She wasn't a dance hall girl, her costume showed that. She wore faded Levis that didn't fail to set off the enticing curves of her trim little form. Her eyes were wide and darkly blue, her lips vividly red, her hair brown and inclined to curl. It was Mary Morales.

"Something must be wrong," muttered Jennings. He jumped to his feet and strode over to where the girl stood. A moment later he led her to the table and procured a chair for her.

"She's looking for the sheriff," he explained to Hatfield, who had risen to his feet and bared his black head.

"Yes," said the girl. "I must find him. Harry Patton, my range boss, was killed sometime this afternoon."

"Killed?" Hatfield repeated.

"Yes," she said, her red lips trembling. "Murdered! Shot through the back of his head. One of the boys found him on my west range, near the cliffs. I must notify the sheriff."

"You stay right here with Jim and I'll hunt up Cobert," Jennings said. "Street sort of wooly for a girl to be out alone tonight."

Before she could object, he was headed for the door. Hatfield and the girl were left gazing at each other. He knew that she had instantly recognized him. She was the first to speak.

"I'm sorry over the way I ran off the other day," she said. "But what you told me upset me terribly. I just had to get away and think. My mind was in a whirl."

"Not illogical, under the circumstances," Hatfield admitted.

"I didn't even learn your name," she said.

Hatfield's mouth tightened a little. "Ma'am," he said, "let's stop playing. You know very well that I am Jim Hatfield and a Ranger."

"A Ranger!" she repeated, her eyes widening. "But what makes you think I should know that?"

"Rather logical to believe that Robert Morales would have told you," Hatfield remarked dryly.

She gazed at him wonderingly. "Mr. Hatfield," she said, "I haven't seen my cousin Robert Morales for more than five years."

It was Hatfield's turn to look startled. "You mean he hasn't been coming to your place since he got back to this section?" he asked incredulously.

The blue eyes met his squarely. "That's just what I mean," she said. "If he had, the chances are I wouldn't be here telling you about it."

"What do you mean by that?" he asked.

"As I said, I have not seen him for more than five years, but I have heard from him. I got a letter from him about four years ago. A bitter, recriminatory letter. He accused me of stealing the property that was rightly his. That I was no better than the men who robbed his father. He ended by

103

promising to come back sometime and kill me. He meant it! I have lived in terror ever since I heard he was back. And when you told me it was he who dropped you over the cliff, it was a considerable jolt to learn he had been so close to my ranchhouse, within sight of it, in fact."

There was a ring of sincerity in her voice that made it impossible for him to doubt her. His lips pursed in a soundless whistle. Here was a nice complication indeed.

"You said your range boss was killed this afternoon? Do you feel that Robert Morales was responsible?"

"Who else?" she asked bitterly. "Poor Harry didn't have an enemy in the world, so far as I ever heard. Everybody liked him. And he testified in my favor at the court hearing when the Walking R was awarded to me. He testified that Uncle John, Robert's father, had told him that he intended leaving the property jointly to Robert and me. Which, I think, influenced Judge Donavan in making his decision."

Hatfield nodded thoughtfully. "And Judge Donavan was killed recently."

"Killed! I thought his horse threw him."

"So most people thought," Hatfield replied grimly. "But you can count on it that he was murdered, and by your cousin Robert."

"He's mad!" she said, her voice quivering. "Utterly insane. When we were together at the ranch he wouldn't have dreamed of doing such a thing. He must be mad."

"I'm inclined to agree with you," Hatfield said. "And now there are two things I want to ask of you, even though I figure I'm pretty deep in your debt already. Nobody here knows I'm a Ranger, except Morales, and I'd like to keep it quiet for a while longer if possible, so please just forget what you told me."

"You don't have to worry," she promised, "I won't talk. What else do you want me to do?"

"Until that crazy hellion is taken care of or out of the section, leave your ranchhouse and come here to town to live or, better still, stay at Cale Jennings' place for a while. He'd be glad to have you."

Her firm little chin went up. "I can't promise that," she said. "I'm frightened, I admit it, but I don't intend to let anybody run me off my property."

"It would be the sensible thing to do," Hatfield urged.

"Perhaps, but I'm not going to do it."

Hatfield swore in exasperation, under his breath. "Women!" he growled. "Why the devil do they always have to be so contrary!"

"Because we're made that way, I guess," she smiled.

"What I should do," he declared morosely, "is turn you across my knee, give you a good spanking and then tuck you under my arm and pack you to the Swinging J ranchhouse and lock you in!"

The blue eyes danced. "Doesn't sound so bad," she replied, "except that this is a terribly public place. It would very likely startle some of the boys sober, and what a waste of time and money that would be for them."

"It's nothing to joke about," he grunted. "Not with that *loco lobo* on your trail."

Mary laughed. "Here comes Mr. Jennings," she said.

Old Cale dropped into a chair, breathing hard, and mopped his heated brow.

"I found Cobert and told him what happened," he said. "He'll be here in a little bit. He's in a place down the street where it 'pears trouble might be building up. He — look out! It's bustin' loose here!"

At the bar, voices had suddenly raised in loud altercation. A big miner knocked a

106

cowhand to the floor with a swinging blow, and was in turn felled by another puncher. Instantly the whole lower end of the bar was a mad tangle of swearing, hitting, kicking, wrestling men. The bartenders uttered soothing yells that were not heeded. Rolf Owens and his floor men rushed forward. Old Cale went storming across the room, shouting to his hands to behave. They didn't.

Mary shrank back in her chair, her face white. "Heavens! it's terrible!" she gasped.

"Nothing serious," Hatfield reassured her. "Just a scuffle. Be a few black eyes and bloody noses, but nothing worse. The floor men will handle it."

The floor men were "handling" it, but it took some time. Several minutes elapsed before they had hurled the bruised and bloody combatants apart to stand muttering and glowering. Old Cale began tongue lashing his men.

Rolf Owens suddenly whirled and rushed to the door of the back room. He fumbled with a key, opened the door and streaked through, leaving it half open behind him. A wrathful shout sounded, the muffled boom of a shot and the thud of a falling body.

Jim Hatfield raced across the room,

hurling men out of his path. He bounded through the door. Owens was on his hands and knees, groveling and cursing. A tall, broad-shouldered figure was just sliding through a second door on the far side of the room. Hatfield jerked his guns and snapped two shots at the man, and knew he had missed. He leaped for the door as a clatter of fast hoofs sounded outside.

But at that moment Rolf Owens surged to his feet directly in the Ranger's path. They met head on and hit the floor together. By the time Hatfield had untangled himself from the raving bar owner the hoof beats were but a whisper of sound in the distance. When he reached the dark alley back of the saloon, nothing was in sight. He swore under his breath, ejected the spent shells from his gun and replaced them with fresh cartridges. Then he went back to the room into which men were crowding and Owens, mopping away the blood that streamed from a gash just above his left temple, was raving tenfold worse than before.

"Did you get the sidewinder?" he yelled at Hatfield.

"He got away," the Ranger answered briefly.

"The mangy sheepherder!" stormed

Owens. "Knocked the combination off the safe and cleaned it. I heard the racket when that infernal row stopped and got in just as he'd finished filling his sack. He cut down on me and creased me. Of all the nerve!"

He whirled to shake a fist at the erstwhile battlers. "Did you horned toads stage that ruckus to cover up for him?" he bellowed.

"Now, now, Rolf," soothed old Cale. "My boys were in that wring. You know they ain't covering up for no owlhoots."

"Well, they sure timed it perfect," snorted Owens.

"Chances are the hellion was standing outside the window watching for his chance," said Jennings. "The ruckus gave it to him, that's all. What do you think, Jim?"

"Sounds logical," Hatfield replied. He spoke calmly, but inwardly he was seething with anger.

"Pulled it right under my nose!" he muttered to himself. "And I'd be willing to bet he knew he was doing just that. Well, he went a considerable way toward recouping the loss of the payroll. Cold, deadly and daring, and never misses a bet. And I thought maybe the luck was due for a change!"

He gazed somberly at the open safe, beside which lay a heavy, short-handled hammer, which had doubtless been used to knock the combination knob off the old box. One quick, hard blow would have done it. He noted that the lock on the back door had also been smashed. The robber had really hardly needed the row at the bar to cover up what little noise he made breaking in. The normal racket going on would doubtless have been sufficient. It was the sudden comparative silence that followed the ending of the ruckus that enabled Owens to hear something going on inside the locked back room.

"Wonder if the hellion will drop in later for a snort?" he growled. "Wouldn't put it past him."

9

Hatfield went back to the table and told Mary what happened.

"It was Robert, wasn't it?" she instantly asked, with feminine intuition.

Hatfield shrugged. "I didn't see his face, but the chore had all the earmarks of his work."

"He has the cunning of the insane," she said, and shivered.

"Well, he's sure got something and plenty of it," Hatfield admitted. "I've a notion it's a regular game with him — all he has to live for — and he's perfectly willing to gamble his life against long odds at any time. And so far he's done a good job of winning."

"But he'll lose in the end," she declared with conviction.

"But a lot of folks are getting hurt meanwhile," Hatfield replied moodily. "He seems to be always just one jump ahead of everybody."

She nodded. "Here comes the sheriff!" she exclaimed. "He looks worried."

"Guess he's got reason to," Hatfield answered dryly.

Jennings intercepted Cobert at the door and they came to the table together. The sheriff swore wearily when informed of the latest depredation.

"Sorry, Mary," he apologized, "but I'm sort of beside myself these days. Is poor Harry's body at the ranchhouse?"

"Yes," she replied, her eyes filling with tears, "the boys brought him in."

"I'll ride out there first thing tomorrow and take Doc McChesney with me," the sheriff promised. "You got a place to sleep tonight? The town's packed and most everything is filled up."

"I had planned to go back —" she began, met Hatfield's eye and did not finish the sentence.

"Why not go out to my place?" Jennings offered. "It's closer and I got plenty of room and you'll have company on the way. If you folks are 'greeable, I'm ready to call it a night right now. Don't figure there'll be any more excitement."

"Suits me," Hatfield agreed. "Come on, Mary."

They rode home under the waning moon, the hills to the south like gray ghost mountains against the stars. Hatfield wondered just where in that shadowy vastness Robert Morales had his hide-out. Would be like hunting for a particular tick on a sheep's back, unless he had the good luck to strike the outlaw's trail away from somewhere, and Morales didn't appear in the habit of leaving any trails he didn't want followed.

Hatfield said goodnight to Jennings and Mary, but he didn't go to bed immediately, late though it was. For a long time he sat by the open window watching the play of the moonlight on the trees and thinking deeply. He was trying to anticipate the outlaw's next move, with scant success. Of course there was the chance that he would hang around the Walking R ranchhouse, waiting for an opportunity to glut his vengeance; but Hatfield could hardly believe that Morales, bad as he was, would go to such lengths to kill a woman. However, he might. No telling just how warped his mind might be.

The dawn was cloudless, fiery red. A wind came out of the northern spruces and the air had an autumn sharpness. Hatfield thrilled to the beauty of the dying year as the strengthening light threw its gleaming mantle over the wide rangeland and flashed the hill crests with molten gold. But his eyes grew heavy and he tumbled into bed, not to awaken until late in the morning.

He found Mary Morales sitting on the porch when he descended the stairs. She greeted him with a smile and a cordial good morning. He sat down on the edge of the porch with his long legs swinging, rolled a cigarette and regarded her gravely though the blue haze of the smoke.

"Reconsidered what you said last night?" he asked. "I hope you have. I can hardly believe Morales would harm a woman, especially his own cousin, but you never can tell about that sort."

"Frankly, I don't think he'd stop at anything once his anger is aroused," she replied. "But I haven't reconsidered. I'm going back to my place as soon as the sheriff arrives. He said he'd come around this way and pick me up."

Hatfield stood up, towering over her. He cupped her chin in his hand and gazed down into her wide eyes. "You're stubborn as a blue-nosed mule," he told her, "but I hope you won't mind if I drop around now and then, just to make sure everything is okay."

"You'll always be welcome, but I think you're more dangerous than Robert Morales."

"Dangerous?"

"Yes, to my peace of mind. Come on, the cook's calling us in to breakfast, and I'm starved."

The coroner's jury ruled that Harry Patton, the Walking R range boss, met his death at the hands of parties unknown, and attached a typical cow country rider to the verdict that advised the sheriff to run down Robert Morales and shoot him on sight.

The sheriff was willing, but he hardly knew where to start. Jim Hatfield was tangled in the same loop: he didn't know where to start.

Hatfield had ridden to the Walking R with the sheriff and Mary Morales. He wanted to familiarize himself with the trail and get a look at the spread. It was fine rangeland, he quickly decided. The buildings were spacious and well cared for. Mary Morales knew the cow business, all right.

"We're getting a big shipping herd together," she told him.

"I have a buyer who is anxious to take everything we can let go. I'm just about stripping the spread of everything salable. I aim to put the money in improved stock."

"You'll end up a rich woman," Hatfield told her. She shrugged her slim shoulders.

"Perhaps," she admitted, "but I'll admit the thought doesn't interest me much. I like the rangeland and the work, but other things interest a woman more."

"What, for instance?"

"A husband and a flock of kids."

"Shouldn't be hard to come by one, or both," Hatfield chuckled.

"First things first," she smiled. "Come again, Jim, and soon."

Hatfield promised he would.

10

The hills to the south interested Hatfield. He felt certain that somewhere in their rugged vastness Morales had his hangout, and not far from Preston. His ability to appear at various points in the vicinity was evidence that he did not have to ride far from some focal spot to a perimeter that included the town and the immediate ranches and trails. It was a logical assumption. The outlaw had doubtless carefully plotted his area of operations so that his hiding place was always within a comparatively short ride from wherever he chose to strike.

That he must have a hangout was fairly obvious. Even an outlaw has to eat and sleep, and doing so in the open for any extended period is fraught not only with discomfort and inconvenience but also with attendant danger. The smoke of a campfire can be seen a long ways unless the builder can always obtain plenty of very dry wood. Which isn't practical in damp weather. This and other considerations make it imperative for him to find some carefully chosen shelter where he can lie snug at all times.

But to try to hunt out the spot, Hatfield knew, verged on the ridiculous. It might be anywhere within the compass of a plot of many square miles. The hills were full of abandoned cabins, shacks and lean-tos built over the course of the years by hunters, trappers, miners, prospectors and desert rats. Any one would serve Morales' purpose, and he would undoubtedly choose one as inaccessible as possible and well hidden. Plenty of such available. There had been outlaws, smugglers, wideloopers and hunted men operating in this section for a century and more. They had built with care and an eye to all possible angles. As old Jennings said, an owlhoot might well lie hidden for an indefinite period if he didn't have to come out to replenish his supplies.

And there was the one weak link in an otherwise almost impervious chain. Morales had to get in and out of the hills.

And the trails running into the wasteland were not numerous. After considerable searching and riding, Hatfield decided that the track that turned south but a few miles from the Walking R ranchhouse was the most likely. He tried riding it for a while, but there were numerous branches running this way and that and he soon gave it up as an impossible chore. His only hope was to catch sight of the outlaw using it, trail him to his hangout or run him down.

This was also fraught with difficulty. Perversely the trail either ran for a long distance through the open where no holeup was available or through such brush grown ruggedness that a rider was not discernible until he was a few hundred feet distant. Finally after considerable searching he hit on a spot that he dubiously decided might do. A hilltop from which he could see the southward trail for several miles.

The place had several disadvantages. For one thing, he could not see the trail to the north and west of the hill. Then, the crest was utterly barren and smooth. No brush, no boulders, nothing that would provide concealment. He himself would be in plain view from the trail below. Added was the fact that there was nearly a mile of rough going from where he sat his horse to the track below. But it was the best that offered. Hatfield took up his post on the crest and resigned himself to tedious watching and waiting.

The first day nothing happened and he rode home tireder than if he had spent the day snaking cows out of bogs. But on the evening of the second day his wearisome vigil was rewarded. A horseman suddenly appeared from the north, riding southward at a good pace. Hatfield did not know whether it was Morales, but he acted on the premise that it was. For certainly nobody could have any legitimate business in the wasteland to the south. He sent Goldy down the slope as fast as the roughness of the sag permitted.

Of course he was instantly spotted by the man below. Hatfield saw him turn in his saddle and gaze up the slope. Then he faced to the front and quickened his horse's gait. Now Hatfield was convinced that it *was* Morales. But by the time he reached the trail, the other had better than a mile lead. Now it was up to Goldy. And the great sorrel responded nobly. He really got down to business and began closing the distance. Hatfield loosened the Winchester in the saddle boot. Soon he would be within rifle range.

But he must hold his fire until absolutely certain that the man ahead was Morales. He could be some harmless puncher who didn't like the looks of the horseman charging down the slope and thought it better to put distance between them. Hatfield intently studied the other as the space between them shortened.

"It's him, horse," he said at length. "No doubt about it. Now if he just doesn't slide into some confounded crack and give us the slip, this ought to be a showdown."

The miles flowed under the sorrel's speeding irons. Hatfield reached for his rifle. And then Morales did turn from the trail and slide into a crack before Hatfield could line sights with him. With an oath the Ranger gave all his attention to riding.

When he reached the crack in question it did not look too discouraging. A rather narrow canyon that bored into the hills, it appeared to be fairly straight, devoid of tall growth. In fact there was practically no chaparral on its level floor. Only a heavy stand of grass so high that the dried heads touched Goldy's belly. And ahead was Morales. Hatfield was encouraged to see that the sides of the canyon were too steep to be negotiated by a horseman. And the loom of hills ahead suggested that the gorge was a box. Perhaps Morales in desperation had decided that here was as good a spot as any to make a stand. Hatfield urged Goldy to greater effort.

Ahead the canyon floor began to slope upward to a crest where the tall grass waved and fluttered in the strong wind that poured down this natural suckhole, fluttering the Ranger's hat and causing him to tighten the chin strap. He was thankful that because of the heavy stand of grass there was no dust for the wind to kick up and blind him. He was rapidly closing the distance and again almost within rifle range when the fugitive topped the sag, rode across the level crest and vanished down the far slope.

Hatfield became very much on the alert as Goldy toiled up the sag. The outlaw might try to hole up in the grass on the crest, but because of the way the wind kept flattening the stand, Hatfield didn't think it likely. He could hardly hope to lie concealed. Nevertheless he took no chances and his eyes never left the flickering crest.

And then abruptly a dark cloud billowed up over the summit of the rise, swirling and writhing in the wind.

"What the devil?" Hatfield muttered,

and instinctively slowed the sorrel. He stared at the thickening cloud, and even as he gazed a golden flood swept over the crest with the billowing smoke cloud above it and raced down the slope.

Hatfield whirled his horse and fled for his life. Morales, with fiendish cunning, had fired the heavy stand of tinder-dry grass. And no horse living can hope to outrun a grass fire with a strong wind behind it, and the draft that soared down the canyon was first cousin to a hurricane.

Goldy, frightened half out of his wits by that roaring, crackling monster at his heels, was giving everything he had; but fast as he traveled, the fire traveled faster.

"If the hellion had waited a couple of minutes longer before setting a match to it, we wouldn't have had a chance," Hatfield muttered. "Going to be touch and go as it is, with the odds against us. Sift sand, horse, if you don't want to be a barbecue!"

Hatfield gagged and choked in the thickening smoke. He was powdered with stinging ash, and the wind that had been refreshingly cool was now as a blast from a furnace. The withering heat sapped his strength and seemed to be drying his blood. And the fire was thundering at their very heels.

Goldy screamed, as only a horse can scream in the last throes of utter terror. The eerie sound caused Hatfield to shiver despite the frightful heat that flowed about him like the waves of a burning sea. He leaned low in the saddle, muffled his neckerchief about his mouth and tried to hold his breath. The smoke was so thick he couldn't see a yard in front of him. He could only let the frantic horse choose his own gait and path. And a fall, or even a stumble would be instantly fatal.

Goldy screamed again as the flames lapped his hind quarters. He gave a tremendous bound and the horror almost upon him inspired one last frantic effort. Hatfield set his teeth and straightened up. This was the end. Might as well take it standing. Abruptly the smoke thinned. The roar of the conflagration lessened. The air freshened. They were fifty yards outside the canyon before Hatfield realized they had escaped a death of torture by the flicker of an eyelash. They were another hundred yards distant from the flames that sputtered out quickly against the sparse, green outer growth before he could pull his utterly demoralized mount to a sobbing, choking halt.

Hatfield dismounted stiffly and tried to

swab some of the grime from his face with his sleeve.

"Feller, you did it," he said, drawing a deep breath of the cool, fresh air. "A minute ago I wouldn't have believed it possible, but you did it."

Goldy stood with legs widespread, head hanging, breathing in shuddering gulps, completely spent. His coat was flecked with foam and caked with ash, his eyes gorged with blood, his mouth open and gasping, his nostrils expanded and he was trembling in every limb. Hatfield loosened the cinches and removed the bit. With water from his canteen he wiped the horse's lips and nostrils. He emptied the container into his hat and allowed him to drink, which he did, painfully and slowly. With the few remaining drops, Hatfield moistened his own parched lips. Then he turned and shook his fist at the smoking canyon. He was not given to gestures, especially futile ones, but under the circumstances he felt one would be permissible. The hair-trigger thinking and devilish ingenuity of Robert Morales was enough to exasperate a saint. No doubt at the moment he was riding comfortably to safety, chuckling over the trick he had played on his pursuer and wondering if he had managed to escape the holocaust he had loosed.

Hatfield allowed the sorrel to rest and regain his strength. Then, scorched, blackened and powdered with ash, he mounted and rode slowly home, thoroughly disgusted with things in general and himself in particular. It was long past sundown when he reached the ranchhouse and everybody had gone to bed, for which he was thankful. He was in no mood for questions and explanations.

11

Three evenings later, when Hatfield rode into the Swinging J ranchhouse after a hard day's work, he saw a corpulent and cheerful individual driving away in a buckboard. At supper Jennings mentioned the man in the buckboard.

"We should start that trail herd we're getting together on the north pasture rolling in a couple of days," he remarked. "John Birdwell, a buyer I've dealt with for quite a few years, was here this afternoon and paid for the critters. He wants all he can get. He was headed for the Walking R when he left here, to pay for Mary Morales' big herd and tell her to hustle 'em along. He had a hefty of dinero in that old gripsack between his feet, but I reckon it's safe enough. Bird's a shrewd article and a salty proposition. Looks harmless but ain't."

Hatfield's black brows drew together as he listened. He finished his supper rather hurriedly. "Think I'll take a little ride," he announced abruptly.

"Okay by me," replied Jennings, "only I'd think you'd had enough after a day in the hull."

"This ride will be different," Hatfield said, and meant it.

Hatfield rode off at a leisurely pace, but once he was out of sight of the ranchhouse, he swiftly quickened Goldy's speed till the great sorrel was racing over the hard trail.

"Sift sand, feller," Hatfield told him. "I'm playing another hunch, and if it happens to be a straight one and that buyer gets to the Walking R *casa* before we do, there'll very likely be another killing tonight. Trail, Goldy! Trail!"

The golden horse responded nobly. His steely legs drove backward like pistons, he slugged his head above the bit, rolled his eyes, snorted and fairly poured his long body over the ground. At each bend they rounded, Hatfield strained his eyes for a glimpse of the buckboard. He counted off the miles, setting the tally against the time that had elapsed since the vehicle left the

Swinging J ranchhouse. If he had only thought to ask Jennings who his visitor was! But he didn't, and there was no use worrying about that now.

The night closed down and it was very dark, with only a ghostly glimmer of starlight throwing a weird sheen across the rolling prairie. A little wind stirred the leaves and the grass heads, making a mournful music, and still there was no dark blotch on the trail ahead. The faint gray ribbon lay lonely and deserted till it merged with the shadows that crowded it on either side. The sorrel's glorious golden coat was stained dark with sweat and flecked white with foam, his breath came in sobbing pants, but his speed never slackened, and ahead was a tall rise beyond which was the Walking R ranchhouse.

They topped the rise and below, a couple of miles distant, lay a dark huddle that marked the *casa* and its surrounding buildings. Hatfield peered ahead and thought he could make out something shadowy and moving not far from the ranchhouse yard. He urged Goldy to greater effort and the sorrel gave his all in one final burst of speed. And Hatfield knew that what he glimpsed was the buckboard entering the ranchhouse yard.

A quarter of a mile from the building he turned Goldy from the trail onto the prairie, where his speeding hoofs would beat but a whisper of sound from the tall and thick grass. He estimated the distance — six hundred yards — four — three — two. Now he could make out the yellow squares of lighted windows. He dared not ride any nearer.

"Easy, feller!" he whispered, pulling back on the reins.

Goldy slowed, came to a panting halt. "Take it easy, now," Hatfield told him and slipped from the saddle. He ran forward, bending low to guard against possible observation.

Suddenly a golden rectangle showed in the dark mass of the ranchhouse; a door had opened. Hatfield caught a fleeting glimpse of a bulky figure outlined against the light before the door closed. He raced forward. He had reached the edge of the yard when he heard the muffled boom of a single shot. He swore bitterly. His hunch had been a straight one, but he was too late.

Not too late to save another life, though, perhaps, and to avenge the one that had just been snuffed out. He sped across the yard, went up the steps at a bound and hit the closed door with his shoulder, with all his two hundred pounds of muscular weight behind it.

The door crashed open and Hatfield was in a lighted room, narrowing his eyes against the glare. Roped to a chair was Mary Morales, a handkerchief tied over her mouth. On the floor lay the body of Birdwell, the buyer, a plump gripsack still clutched in his dead hand. And bending over him, a gun in his hand, was a man who jumped up as Hatfield burst into the room. It was Robert Morales.

Hatfield jerked his gun and fired from the hip as Morales pulled trigger. A slug ripped a red streak across his cheek bone and for an instant the room was filled with dazzling light through which he heard a clang of metal as Morales' gun, its lock smashed by the Ranger's bullet, flew from his hand and thudded on the floor. Before Hatfield could get the stars and comets out of his eyes, Morales had whirled and dashed through an open door.

Hatfield tore after him, along a dark hall, shooting as he ran. He heard another door bang open and felt a gush of cool air. He raced for the opening.

Something hit his knees, hard, and he hurtled through the air as if thrown from a

131

catapult to strike the ground with a force that knocked all the breath from his lungs and half stunned him. As he struggled to get control of his near-paralyzed limbs he heard the beat of fast hoofs fading into the distance. By the time he managed to scramble to his feet, the sound had ceased.

For a moment he stood gasping and retching, trying to pump some air into his lungs, his head still whirling.

"A jump ahead of me again!" he panted wrathfully. "Never misses a bet! Had everything set for a quick getaway if he needed one. Stretched a rope across the back door so that anybody who tried to follow him would take a header! That hellion's too smart to be real!"

There was no way of telling which way the fugitive had gone, and even if he had known it was hopeless to try to catch him with Goldy utterly exhausted by the frantic race from the Swinging J ranchhouse. Hatfield turned and limped back into the house. He pulled the gag from around Mary's mouth and with a couple of slashes of his knife cut the ropes that bound her to the chair. She clung to him, sobbing and moaning. He held her close and smoothed her hair and patted her cheeks till she had recovered something of her self-control.

"Jim, somehow I knew you'd come," she said at last. "I was sure of it, but I was so terribly scared he'd kill you. Did he hurt you much?"

"Only my self-esteem," Hatfield replied. "He just about busted that into humpty-dumpty pieces. You all right?"

"Yes, he didn't hurt me," she replied, "but I think he would have killed me if you hadn't burst in when you did."

"Where are all your hands?" Hatfield asked. "Why didn't somebody come to see who fired that shot?"

"They're all up on the east pasture, guarding the trail herd," she replied. "And the cook and the corral wrangler went to town and didn't come back like they were supposed to. They should have been here hours ago."

Hatfield did not say so, but he grimly suspected that the cook and the wrangler would never come back.

"How did he get in and catch you?" he asked.

"I don't know," she said. "He moves like a shadow. I was in the kitchen and all of a sudden he was beside me. There was a gun in the table drawer. I grabbed for it but he was too quick for me. He seized me and carried me into this room and tied me to the chair. Jim, he's utterly mad; his eyes and his talk showed it plainly. After he tied me, he pulled up a chair and talked. I felt that he just had to talk to someone. It was like a pent-up flood bursting loose. He told me all about the years he'd been away, the crimes he had committed, the places he'd been. It was a veritable Odyssey of evil adventure. Seems he'd spent considerable time in Mexico and there is a place there he kept referring to. He called it *Valle de las Estrellas.*"

"Starlight Valley," Hatfield translated.

"Yes. The place seemed to hold a fascination for him; he spent nearly a year there, I gathered. He spoke of a ranch there he wanted to own. I think there he found something like peace and I believe he very nearly decided to go straight. But the urge for vengeance was too strong. It brought him back here. When he talked of that valley and things there, his eyes got soft and dreamy like they were when I first knew him. But when he turned to his desire for vengeance on those he believed had wronged him, the mad glitter came back to them and his face twisted and contorted. He said he was about ready to pull out of here, now that he'd done everything he'd planned to do. He was just waiting to grab off the money he knew the buyer was carrying. He seems obsessed with a desire for a lot of money, to finance some secret plan he has in mind. He intimated that he was going to Arizona from here and mentioned a place called Galeyville and a San Simon Valley where he said there are rich pickings and boasted that a man need little fear the law, especially if he was in with the right people."

"Near Tombstone," Hatfield interpolated. "A notorious hangout of outlaws."

She nodded. "But I think he is afraid of you, Jim," she said. "I think that is his real reason for leaving the section. His face had a queer, baffled, uncertain look when he spoke of you. He complained that you always escaped him and always turned up just at the wrong moment. Yes, I think he fears you."

"I hope you're right," Hatfield observed somberly.

"I'm sure I am," she said, "and what he told me of his plans made me sure he intended to kill me before he left. He would hardly divulge them if he expected me to remain alive to speak of them."

"Perhaps," Hatfield admitted, "and then perhaps not. A deranged mind takes some funny turns. He may feel that where he intends to go he will be safe and that perhaps I wouldn't follow him there. It's not in Texas and I'm a Texas law officer. Hard to tell just how he reasons."

"Perhaps," she repeated after him, and did not look convinced. "Anyhow, I feel sure he's leaving, for which I am thankful, for my own sake and for yours. It would appear we have both escaped his vengeance."

"Maybe," Hatfield replied, "but I agree with you that he's very likely to pull out. What happened tonight must have given him considerable of a jolt. It's just luck that he and I both are alive. Both slugs came mighty close to making a finish job of it."

"Do you think you hit him while you were shooting in the hall?" she asked.

"Not likely," Hatfield replied. "He never stopped going and I didn't see any blood spots. No, I think he made a clean getaway. Well, we both came through satisfactorily, which is more than can be said for that poor devil on the floor. He got it dead center."

"Yes," she said with a shudder. "Robert shot him right after he opened the door and let him in. He must have ears like a dog, because he heard the buckboard wheels long before I did. All of a sudden he cocked his head in an attitude of listening, then he whipped out a handkerchief and gagged me with it so I couldn't scream a warning. It was horrible! And when he talked of his vengeance, I felt as if a cold hand was gripping my heart and wondered what the 'Other Side' would be like when I got there."

"A harrowing experience," Hatfield agreed. "Well, all's well that ends well, even if the ending is only temporary. Guess I might as well take care of poor Birdwell."

He stooped and raised the buyer's heavy body, apparently without effort, and placed it on a couch. Mary procured a blanket and Hatfield drew a fold over the dead face.

"Hope you're not afraid to stay in the house with him," he observed.

Mary shook her head. "I never had any fear of the dead," she replied. "The dead can't hurt you; it's the living you must watch out for."

"Smart girl," nodded Hatfield. "Now guess I'd better go look after my horse; he was pretty well all in."

"You're not going to leave me here alone tonight, are you?" she asked.

"Of course not," he assured her. "I'm

going to stay right with you," he added, smoothing her hair.

She colored prettily and glanced up at him through the silken fringe of her lashes. "Then I'll feel perfectly safe," she said softly.

Hatfield chuckled and left the ranchhouse. He gave Goldy a good rubdown, stalled him comfortably in the stable and made sure that all his wants were provided for. When he returned to the house, he found Mary busy in the kitchen preparing hot coffee and something for them to eat. Later they left a low light burning in the room where Birdwell lay and ascended the stairs together.

As Hatfield predicted, the cook and the wrangler did not show up during the night. Doubtless Morales, who appeared to know everything and see everything that went on, had taken care of that little detail. But two punchers rode in from the night-guard shortly after breakfast. Hatfield sent one riding to town to notify the sheriff of the murder of Birdwell. "And tell him to pick up Cale Jennings and bring him along," he directed.

"And I guess there's no sense in me keeping up a pretense in this section any longer — it's outlived its usefulness," he told Mary as he took his Ranger's star from the secret pocket in his belt and pinned it on his shirt front. "Later it may be a good notion to go undercover again."

"You're going to follow him?" she asked, her pupils dilating.

"Of course," Hatfield replied simply. "I was handed the chore of running him down and putting a stop to his criminal activities. So far I haven't been able to do either. He has broken Texas law and must be held accountable."

"I suppose so," she agreed, "but I can't help but be afraid for you. He is terrible."

"Oh, maybe I'll get the breaks next time," Hatfield said lightly. "It's a long worm that has no turning."

"I don't see how you can joke about it," she protested. "It's a serious matter and you're taking your life in your hands."

"Maybe," he admitted. "You took yours in your hands when you slid down that rope the other day. Didn't seem to bother you."

"That was different," she replied. "I had to do what I could to save you."

"And I have to do what I can to save others," he pointed out. "Life is uncertain at best. Those it would seem should live a long time sometimes don't. I have reason to know." He gazed out the window, his eyes somber.

Her hand tightened on his and she regarded him with deeply understanding eyes.

"I think you must have a strong religious streak," she said.

"A man who doesn't have isn't much good to the world, nor to himself, either," he replied. "And it isn't bad to have. Somebody to go to when the going seems to be getting too rough. I hope I'll always be that way."

"You will," she declared with conviction.

Sheriff Cobert was goggle-eyed when he saw the star on Hatfield's breast, but Cale Jennings didn't appear overly surprised.

"Sort of had a notion about it for some time," he said. "I know how Rangers work. And Jess Mosman just about spotted you after he thought things over a while. He figured from the beginning that he'd seen you somewhere, and it finally come to him. You're the Lone Wolf, aren't you?"

"Been called that," Hatfield admitted with a smile.

Sheriff Cobert stared in awe at the legendary figure whose exploits were famous throughout the Southwest.

"And Bill McDowell sent you here to

run down Morales?" Jenning pursued.

"That's the general notion," Hatfield replied, "only he's mostly been running me down."

"You've done more than anybody else ever has been able to," said Jennings. "You busted up a couple of his tries, anyhow. And you think he may be leaving the section?"

"I think he is," Hatfield nodded.

"Well, that's good news for us folks here and bad for some other section," declared Jennings. "And you're going after him?"

"I am," Hatfield stated.

"Good hunting!" said Jennings. "I hate to lose the best tophand I ever had, but maybe you'll drop in and see us sometimes."

"It's very likely that I will," Hatfield answered, with a smile that caused Mary Morales to blush.

Three days later, Jim Hatfield sat in the office at Ranger Post headquarters and talked with Captain McDowell.

"I'll get you all the authority you'll need in New Mexico or Arizona," Captain Bill promised. "No trouble about that. And extradition papers if you have use for 'em."

"I doubt if any authority will do me any good other than that I'll pack on my hip,"

Hatfield said. "It is highly unlikely that Morales will allow himself to be taken alive."

"Just the same it's best to have the law behind you," replied the Captain. "But that does put you at a disadvantage," he grumbled. "As I said before, you have to announce yourself instead of going in with both guns blazing. If you'd done that, I've a notion you'd have downed the side-winder the first time you went up against him."

"Maybe," Hatfield said. "We'll see."

"You figure to try and pick up his trail?"

Hatfield shook his head. "Doubtful if I could do it," he answered. "He'll cover up. No, I'm going to follow the tip Mary Morales gave me concerning his plans. I'm heading straight for the San Simon Valley. I figure I should be able to get a line on him in Tombstone or Galeyville. He may tie up with one of the outfits in Galeyville or Charleston, but I doubt it. It appears he has always worked alone and there's little reason to believe he'll change now. He evidently is well acquainted with the section and knows where he'll have a chance to make good hauls. Tombstone is a booming silver town and there are also strikes around Charleston and Galeyville. No railroad there and stages must pack plenty of dinero. A shrewd and salty hellion like Morales should find plenty of opportunities to fill his poke. I'll try and keep under cover and maybe I can get a line on him before he gets one on me, like he did at Preston. Oh, he's got plenty of savvy, and, unlike most of his brand, he looks ahead. I think he plans in detail every move he intends to make, and once he starts he goes like chain lightning."

"Well, my money's still on the Lone Wolf," said Captain Bill.

"Hope you don't go busted," chuckled Hatfield.

12

On a golden afternoon in early October, a
tall, broad-shouldered, level-eyed Texan
rode up to the Roofless Dobe ranchhouse in
the San Simon Valley. Anybody with half an
eye could tell he was a Texan from his rig.
He rode a lowhorned, clumsy looking Texas
saddle. It had two cinches, the rear one a
piece of stiff leather, the front one of horse-
hair, neither more than three inches wide.
Instead of the long, flexible latigos of soft
whang leather prized by Arizonians, he
merely had a heavy leather strap, like a trunk
strap. When his saddle needed tightening, he
did not have to get down and work on the
latigos with their fancy loops. He simply
leaned over, grabbed his trunk strap, pulled
it up a notch or two and caught the tongue
of the buckle in the hole. The double-cinch

saddle stayed put once it was cinched up, and it did not cut the poor horse in two. His reins were long, heavy, inch-wide straps, not tied together but each independent of the other. Instead of tying his horse with a hair rope, he merely dropped the two strap reins on the ground and the well-trained animal would not move while the split reins trailed. On the saddle, he carried a common sisal rope, one end tied hard and fast to the saddle horn.

Curly Bill Brocius, leader of the boldest and most powerful outlaw organization the Southwest ever knew, owned the Roofless Dobe. He wasn't there at the moment; he was in Galeyville, where he spent most of his time. His range boss, Milt Hicks, lounged on the front porch.

"Light off, feller, and feed your tapeworm," Hicks invited with the ready hospitality of the West. "Look like you've done some riding."

"Considerable," admitted the newcomer in a low, deep voice. He unforked, towering over Hicks, who was himself a six-footer and better.

"Some horse you got," Hicks said admiringly. "As fine a golden sorrel as I ever laid eyes on. Don't suppose you want to sell him?"

"You want to sell your right arm?"

"Nope," replied Hicks. "I'll call a wrangler to put him up."

"Reckon I'd better 'tend to that," said the stranger. "Wrangler might lose part of his hand if he tried to touch him."

Hicks nodded. "I like that kind," he said. "Me for a one-man horse every time. But you'd better keep an eye on him in this section. Somebody might steal him."

"Been tried," the other said shortly.

"And you still got him," chuckled Hicks. "From Texas, ain't you?"

"That's right."

"Whereabouts in Texas?"

"That's my business."

"Uh-huh, reckon it is," nodded Hicks. "Well, put up your critter. Everything you'll need right inside the barn door. Soap and water and towels in back. We eat in ten minutes."

He watched the tall Texan head for the barn with a speculative eye.

"Now wonder where the deuce he came from, and why?" he mused. " 'Peared to have come darn fast. Salty looking jigger. Two-gun man. And those irons are worn in a way that says business. Slung mighty low and to the front. Hmmm! We're getting all sorts hereabouts of late, but that one looks

146

sort of like the he-wolf of the pack. Got a notion he'll interest Bill, if he takes a notion to hang around. Chances are he'll trail his twine, though, after a couple of surroundings and a night's sleep in a bed. And very likely a few days later a sheriff or a Ranger will drop in to ask questions about him."

When the stranger entered the big kitchen, the Roofless Dobe outfit was already seated.

"Here's a gent who 'lows he could stand a helping," Hicks announced. "Make room, boys."

The boys made room, glancing expectantly at the newcomer.

"Hatfield's the name," he complied. "First handle kind of whittled down to Jim."

The boys ducked their heads. Hicks rattled off a number of names, including Joe Hill, Jim Hughes, Jake Gauze, Charlie Turner and Charlie Snow. Hatfield acknowledged the introductions, and it interested the observant Hicks to note that during the meal when he had occasion to address a man, he instantly called him by the right name.

The Roofless Dobe hands had the look of good cowmen and they were a rollicking, jovial lot and good company. But Hatfield knew well that they were also as vicious a band of cutthroats as ever assembled at one table. But he was at the Roofless Dobe from choice, having decided it was the best base of operations to be hit on.

After the meal was eaten and a cigarette or two smoked, Hicks bent a discerning glance on his guest. "Feller," he said, "if you hanker for a little ear pounding, don't wait on us. Take the first room at the head of the stairs and get your shuteye. And remember, anybody that sleeps under this roof ain't got anything to worry about from anybody else under it, and that goes for his belongings, too."

Hatfield nodded his understanding. It was the code of the outlaw fraternity. Once away from the Roofless Dobe he was fair game for anybody who had designs on his person or his horse. But while he was a guest he would receive every consideration and could rest with an easy mind. He thanked Hicks and went to bed and to the first real sleep he'd had in a week.

While he slept he got an unexpected break that he didn't know about until some time later. A couple of hours after dark, Zwig Grounds, one of Curly Bill's lieutenants, rode in from Galeyville. He had considerable news of interest including one item that instantly attracted the attention of Milt Hicks.

"Feller held up the Benson stage last night just about dark," he announced. "Shot the driver and the guard. Just rode out of the brush and started shooting. Didn't say a word till he had 'em both on the ground. Then he called the passengers out — six of 'em, cleaned 'em and made them hand out the strongbox. Box had considerable dinero in it, I gathered. Was a smooth piece of work, all right."

"What sort of a feller?" asked Hicks.

"Tall, broad-shouldered feller packing two guns," said Grounds. "Somebody said he had black hair."

"Anybody notice what color horse he was riding?"

"It was getting pretty dark and I reckon those passengers were too scairt to notice much of anything straight, but I rec'lect a feller saying he rode a light-colored horse, which could mean most anything. All the descriptions were pretty sketchy. About all they agreed on was that the feller shot mighty fast and straight and talked soft but meant what he said. I gathered nobody saw fit to argue with him. Which was showing good judgment, I figure. Feller made a passenger get on the box and take the stage on down the road. He faded into the brush. Sheriff Johnny Behan and Wyatt Earp, Deputy Breckenridge and some others rode out there this morning but didn't find nothing. Feller didn't 'pear to leave any tracks."

"Hmmm!" remarked Hicks, speculatively, "big tall feller, packed two guns and rode a light-colored horse. Hmmn!"

"Some of the passengers 'lowed it might be Doc Holliday and some of his bunch, maybe Bill Leonard and Harry Head," continued Grounds, "but I don't think so. In the first place Holliday had a pretty good alibi that put him sixteen miles away at the time, and in the second place, it sure looked like the feller was working alone. No signs of anybody else around 'less they were squatted in the brush, and that would be a funny way to run a holdup."

"Got a notion you're right," said Hicks. "Hmmm!"

In fact, there was no doubt in Milt Hicks' mind but that the Texan who called himself Jim Hatfield was the man who held up the stage on the Benson road. And it was not unnatural that Hatfield rose in the

150

estimation of Hicks, an outlaw in good standing.

Hicks, of course, would never have thought of asking Hatfield anything relative to the stage holdup. Such things just weren't done. He knew that his question as to where in Texas he had ridden from was ill-advised, and he hadn't been at all offended by the short answer he got. Where a man came from was his own business, where he was going more so. So the following morning, when they were enjoying a cigarette after breakfast, Hicks' manner was elaborately casual when he asked —

"Just passin' through?"

"Sort of depends," Hatfield replied. "Feller can't eat if he doesn't work, or so I've been told."

"Consider a job of riding?"

"I might, of the right sort of riding."

"I can use another tophand," suggested Hicks.

Hatfield smoked in silence for a moment, then, " 'Pears to be a rather nice section. Have much trouble with wideloopers hereabouts?"

"Some," Hicks admitted.

"Suppose the sheriff runs 'em down pronto."

Hicks grinned. "Sheriff don't seem to

take much interest in things over this-a-way," he replied. "Johnny Behan mostly stays in Tombstone. Pretty lively pueblo, Tombstone, and keeps him sort of busy."

Hatfield nodded. "Reckon I'll sign up," he said.

"Good!" exclaimed Hicks. "You won't regret it, feller, this is the best outfit in the section to work for. We pay better than average wages — for regular ranch work — and now and then a little bonus on the side, when a feller earns it."

Understanding perfectly what Hicks meant by a "bonus," Hatfield nodded.

"I could use a little extra dinero," he said.

13

Hatfield was assigned routine duties which he performed with efficiency and dispatch, showing the Arizonians things about cattle handling.

"That big Texan sure knows the cow business," chuckled Joe Hill. "He does things the easy way and the fast way. Did you notice how he snakes a horse out of the remuda? No whirling a wide loop for him, and stirring up the whole bunch till they're a milling riot. He sneaks up on 'em like a black man raiding a chicken coop and with his loop lying flat on the ground he gives it an underhand throw and drops it over the neck of the critter he wants. Does it so fast and easy and quiet the rest never stop cropping grass, and that cayuse he's after has a rig on him and is at work before he figures out just what's happened. Yep, that jigger can sure dab a loop!"

It was inevitable that Hatfield would hear about the Benson road holdup, the incident being a prime topic of conversation at the time. He listened intently to the stories told, did not comment but drew his own conclusion.

"So the hellion's here and already working," he mused. "That job has all the earmarks of a Morales' chore: shoot first and say 'hands up!' afterward. Working alone, as has always been his habit. Glad of that. Easier to drop a loop on one man, even if that man is Robert Morales, than to try to corral a whole bunch. And these native grown specimens here are smart and plenty salty."

There were plenty of cows on the Roofless Dobe spread, some of them without any visible brands, many with "skillet-of-snakes" burns that held a meaning only south of the Mexican Border. Hatfield noted this but gave it little thought. That the majority of the Roofless Dobe critters were widelooped was plainly apparent. But he was not an Arizona peace officer and such matters came within the scope of local authorities, and it was up to them to handle them, if they desired to, which apparently they did not. The proof of Curly Bill's political tie-ups was easy to see. All of which did not interest the Lone Wolf. He was in Arizona for a definite purpose and didn't intend to be diverted by extraneous matters.

Riding into the ranchhouse rather early one afternoon a few days after he started working for Hicks, Hatfield found the place in an uproar. Hicks was tending a near-exhausted, half-starved and parched man, his clothes torn to rags by cactus and briers. He was Harry Earnshaw, one of Curly Bill's followers and a friend and neighbor of notorious Old Man Clanton.

Hatfield got the story of what had happened from Jake Gauze, who was too excited to reflect that he was relaying rather dubious information to a comparative stranger who had not as yet been put to the test.

The chain of events leading up to the latest tragedy began about a month before. Curly Bill and some of his men had ambushed a Mexican smuggling train in Skeleton Canyon and rifled the rawhide aparejos, as the packsacks borne by mules were called, of more than seventy thousand dollars in Mexican silver, killing nineteen Mexicans as a little attendant incident.

One Mexican had escaped to carry the news south. It was common knowledge that the relatives of the slain men had vowed vengeance. The Brocius outfit had been very much on the alert, not discounting the seriousness of such a blood feud.

Those taking part in the raid, according to Gauze, were Curly Bill, Old Man Clanton, two of his sons, Ike and Billy, Tom and Frank McLowery, John Ringo, Joe Hill, Jim Hughes, Rattlesnake Bill, Jake Gauze himself, Charlie Thomas and Charlie Snow. The participants had squandered their spoils among the bars of Galeyville, Charleston and Tombstone in true outlaw style.

Naturally the money didn't last long. The outlaws began running low on funds. So six of Bill's men set out upon a cattle raid into Mexico, a few days before Hatfield signed up with the Roofless Dobe. The raid was successful and they rounded up three hundred head and drove them back across the Line. But in the Animas Valley just over the Arizona line in New Mexico, following Mexicans caught up with them. A running fight ensued and the Mexicans recaptured the stolen cattle. Curly Bill, at Roofless Dobe, got word of what had happened. He and a number of his bunch set out after the Mexicans. They caught up with them in San Luis Pass and another running fight ensued. The upshot of the matter was Curly Bill got the cattle back and fourteen more Mexicans died in the blazing gun battle. The score was getting rather one-sided.

The bewildered cows were driven to the Double Dobe ranch owned by Charlie Green and Charles Thomas, two of Curly Bill's henchmen. There they were bought by Old Man Clanton for fifteen dollars a head, Clanton knowing he could sell them at a good profit in Tombstone.

Clanton set out to drive the herd to Tombstone. With him were Dick Gray, Billy Lang, Bud Snow, Harry Earnshaw and Jim Crane. His route would be from Animas Valley through Guadalupe Canyon, where he made his first camp.

The night passed peacefully enough, according to Earnshaw and the camp was astir before dawn. Dick Gray and Jim Crane began kindling a fire. Old Man Clanton stood beside it, warming his hands. Bud Snow and Billy Lang were not yet out of their blankets.

"All of a sudden hell busted loose," said Earnshaw. "Rifle bullets just streamed from the brush on the slope above the camp. Clanton went into the fire, dead as a doornail. The bullets kept coming. Down went Jim Crane, yelling and groaning. Gray tried to run but a slug knocked him into the fire. He kicked most of it out before he died. Bud Snow and Billy Lang piled out of their blankets half asleep. Then Snow laid down again on his blankets, like he'd decided to sleep some more, but he didn't do any snoring. Lang tried to scramble up the rocks but a slug knocked him over like a plugged rabbit.

"Me? I was riding last night guard and that saved me. I sent my pony for the canyon mouth fast as he could go. Wasn't but a hundred yards or so from the camp and just rounding a bend when a slug drilled the cayuse dead center. Down he went, shooting me over his head. I hit mighty hard and was just able to crawl into a clump of brush. I hunkered down there praying none of them goldarn Mexicans would come my way. Nobody did. I heard the cows start moving up the canyon, away from me. I didn't take no chances. Somebody might be hanging back to keep an eye on things. I stayed right where I was till long after the sun was up. Didn't hear a sound up the canyon and knew the boys were all dead. Finally I snuk out of the brush and headed for here. Thought I'd die before I made it. Give me another drink."

The story was received with bitter oaths and vows of vengeance. After making Earnshaw comfortable, Hicks suggested that they ride to the canyon and bring in the bodies.

"Want to come along, Hatfield?" he asked. Hatfield signified that he did and they set out, eight riders and led horses upon which to pack in the bodies.

When they reached the canyon they found that Earnshaw hadn't exaggerated. Five men lay sprawled in or around the scattered fire. The trail of the missing cows led up the canyon. After cursing the Mexicans some more, Hicks followed the herd a little ways.

Jim Hatfield, whose keen eyes missed nothing, quickly discovered something that he wondered why the others had missed. The explanation was simple, however. His companions were so positive that the deed had been done by vengeance seeking Mexicans that they gave scant attention to signs. But Hatfield noted that among the numerous cow tracks were the prints of but a single horse. *One* man only had driven the herd away from the ill-fated camp. Which made it practically certain the one man did all the shooting.

Three hundred cows are a chore for one man to handle, but Hatfield knew it could be done by a really expert driver. The encroaching walls of the canyon would keep the herd bunched until the critters got over their fright. After that they could be shoved along by a single capable rider. What he wanted to know more than anything else was where Robert Morales had disposed of the herd. He determined to find out.

After riding a little ways, Hicks observed disgustedly, "No sense in following those cows. They're way down in Mexico by now. Come on, we'll go back and pack the bodies to the spread. We'll even up with those hellions some day. And it's going to be just too bad for *any* Mexican the Clanton boys meet out on the range from now on."

It was.

After the first few days, Milt Hicks, recognizing a tophand when he saw one, had given Hatfield free rein to handle his work as he saw fit. Hatfield knew that the range boss was studying him and trying to decide just how he might fit into the Brocius organization, but he did not think that Hicks would broach the subject until he had consulted with Curly Bill and John Ringo. Meanwhile, he was left largely on his own except for general orders.

That night, after they had returned to the ranchhouse, Hicks suggested that the next day it might be a good notion to do some combing of the canyons on the southwest range and try and learn how many head were holed up there. Which fitted well with Hatfield's plans.

Mid-morning of the following day found him in Guadalupe Canyon at the site of Clanton's camp. The trail of the thrice-lifted herd was easy to follow. The lone driver had made no effort toward concealment. Doubtless Morales, with his uncanny ability for gathering information, knew just where suspicion would be directed and had no fear of being tracked. For Hatfield had not the least doubt but it was Morales who had pulled the chore.

On leaving the canyon, the trail turned sharply northwest. Hatfield followed it for three hours across barren ground. Finally the nature of the soil changed and he was riding over good rangeland on which grazed a few nondescript looking cows. Another hour and he sighted a ramshackle ranchhouse that boasted an unusually large cattle corral now empty but showing indubitable signs of having been recently occupied by a large number of beefs.

Hatfield recognized the place for what it was — the hangout of a buyer of stolen cattle who would later sell the beefs to a reservation or other lucrative market where no questions were asked. And the trail led to the empty corral.

A lanky man with mis-mated eyes sat on the ranchhouse porch. Hatfield noted that a rifle leaned against a nearby post within reach of his hand. He waved a friendly greeting, however, and called —

"Light off and cool your saddle. Just getting ready to eat."

Hatfield accepted the invitation, sat down on the edge of the porch and rolled a cigarette. The man eyed him speculatively.

"Texan?" he stated, rather than asked.

Hatfield nodded.

"Located in the section?" the man asked.

"For the present," Hatfield replied.

"Good section," said the other. "Figuring on squattin' long?"

"All depends," Hatfield parried. "Doesn't seem so bad."

The lanky man nodded, and fell silent. Hatfield put forth a question of his own.

"Rode over your range getting here," he announced. "Good land, but doesn't 'pear to be over-well stocked."

"I ain't got many critters right now," the other conceded.

"Interested in buying a few?" Hatfield asked.

The other's face did not move a muscle.

"Ain't got overmuch money to invest right now," he said, with just enough uncertainty in his voice to invite further discussion.

Hatfield risked a long shot in the dark.

"My partner sold you three hundred head the other day," he said, looking straight to the front. "Remember him? Tall, broad-shouldered feller with yellow hair. We were satisfied with your price."

The lanky man's face became as expressionless as a wooden platter. He rasped his unshaven chin with a grimy forefinger.

"Can't recall any gent who looked just like that," he observed with elaborate unconcern, too elaborate for a man telling the truth, Hatfield thought. "Sure his hair wasn't black?"

Hatfield slanted his eyes sideways at the fellow and grinned a little. "Could be I'm getting color blind of late," he said.

The other chuckled. "Money's sort of

tight right now," he said, "but I might be interested in a few hundred head. Twenty a head is about the best I could do, though."

"I'll think on it," Hatfield answered. "May see you in a few days."

A dirty and very ornery looking Mexican appeared in the doorway and grunted.

"Come on and eat," said the lanky man, rising to his feet. "You must be hungry after a long ride."

"Reckon I can stand a surrounding," Hatfield admitted.

The food was plentiful and surprisingly well prepared. Hatfield ate heartily and enjoyed his meal. He smoked a cigarette, said goodbye to his host and rode back the way he came. He could feel the lanky man's mis-mated eyes boring into his back and was relieved when he got beyond rifle range.

Nevertheless he was pleased with the day's work. He was convinced that here was where Robert Morales disposed of the stolen herd, clearing around six thousand dollars on the transaction. Which was not bad for a night's work. Widelooping was profitable in Arizona, especially for a rustler of Morales' calibre. The chances were good that he would lift another bunch of cows at the first opportunity.

"And if I can just hear about it in time, I'll know right where to look for the side-winder," he mused. "Which is a hell of a sight more than I know now."

When Hatfield got back to the Roofless Dobe ranchhouse, late in the evening, he found two new arrivals there. He instantly recognized both from many descriptions.

One was a big burly man with curly black hair and snapping black eyes. He had a hearty, jovial manner that was not assumed; but Hatfield knew that Bill Brocius or Graham, as he sometimes called himself, could be a devil incarnate when aroused.

The other was a tall and exceedingly handsome man whose dark face contrasted with his blond hair. He had somber eyes and a soft, cultivated voice. This was the famous John Ringo, the "brains" of the Brocius outfit, a man splendidly brave, chivalrous, educated and cultured, who had thrown his life away and was constantly tortured by regrets and self-condemnation.

"How are you, Hatfield?" Curly Bill said heartily after Hicks had performed the introductions. "Milt tells me you're a tophand from way back. We need that sort hereabouts. Hope you'll stick with us.

Drop over to Galeyville and see me soon. Like to have a talk with you."

He turned to Hicks. "Milt," he said, "the McLowery brothers had a run-in with Wyatt Earp the other day. That sort of thing is going to end in big trouble sooner or later. I've warned 'em to stay out of Tombstone, but they will go. They'd better stay in Galeyville where it's peaceable."

"Anybody killed in Galeyville lately?" Hicks asked cheerfully.

"Funny, that brings something to mind," said Brocius, chuckling. "Funniest thing I've seen in a long while. I'll tell you about it. Remember that big New Mexico cowhand who's been hanging around for a spell — Cal Houck, he called himself?"

"Yep, I remember him," said Hicks. "*Muy malo hombre*. He's one of the fastest men on the draw I ever saw."

"*Was* one," corrected Curly Bill. "Well, Houck came into that little place across the street from Babcock's. I was in there, talking with Billy Claibourne. Houck had been drinking and was ugly, uglier than usual. You could see he hankered for trouble. There was a young feller at the end of the bar who'd dropped in a little before for a quiet drink. Looked a little like a Mexican except for his yellow hair. Some

166

folks 'lowed he is a Mexican, but he ain't. I heard him order his drink and no Mexican speaks English like that.

"Houck looked around, grumbled to himself and swagger-footed to the end of the bar.

" 'Out of my way, oiler,' he says and jostles that young feller. Feller stepped back a little; rather he sort of slid back, moving like he was on springs. He didn't say anything, just looked at Houck, and he's got a pair of eyes that go through you like a greased knife. Houck didn't like it.

" 'Don't look at me like that, oiler!' he bellers, and goes for his gun."

"And then what happened?" asked Hicks, sitting on the edge of his chair.

"What happened? That yellow-haired feller pulls a gun and shoots Houck dead before he can even clear leather. Then he looks around the room, sort of slow and easy like. Nobody said anything. Nobody made a move. I had both of my hands on the table top and believe me, I kept 'em there. Then the feller did a funny thing. He looked down at Houck and said, real soft and low, *'Buenos noches, Senor!'* leathers his gun and walks out. A minute later we heard him riding out of town. Didn't nobody follow him. But what did he mean by that 'Good night, Sir' to a dead man?"

A little later, figuring that the outlaw chief might have something confidential to say to Hicks, Hatfield said goodnight and went up to his room. He'd already heard all he wanted to hear.

After the door at the head of the stairs closed, Hicks turned to Brocius. "Well?" he asked expectantly. "Well, what do you think of him?"

"Well, John, what do you think?" Brocius countered.

"I think," Ringo replied quietly, "that we've been looking at the most dangerous man that ever stepped on Arizona soil."

14

Hatfield considered the information he had gathered from Curly Bill important. What had been guesswork was now fact. Morales was in the section, and there was no longer any doubt but it was Morales who robbed the Benson stage and ran off Old Man Clanton's cattle. Very significant was his presence in Galeyville. Perhaps he was in the habit of visiting the outlaw capital. The same held good for Tombstone, Charleston and Paradise. At last he had something of an idea where to look for the outlaw.

But he still pinned his hopes on the buyer at the out-of-the-way ranch. If he could just hear of one of Morales' raids in time, he'd head straight for the place in the hope of intercepting him there. Also it might be advisable to keep tabs on the ramshackled ranchhouse on the chance that Morales would show up there to discuss business matters with the buyer.

Hatfield also debated the advisability of a visit to Galeyville in the near future. He felt that Brocius was contemplating him as a possible recruit for his outfit, and that the invitation he had extended was in the nature of a feeler.

The notion had certain attractions. As a member of the outlaw fraternity in good standing, many otherwise closed channels of information would be open to him. Such a man as Morales could not continue to operate in the section without attracting the attention of the Brocius bunch, and with its far-flung organization it would sooner or later get a line on him. He was, in a sense, a competitor, and competition always interested the organized outlaws. Their tactic was to assimilate or exterminate it. Hatfield was certain that Morales would not be assimilated; he had always been a lone wolf and would doubtless remain such. And there would likely be certain preliminary difficulties in exterminating him. He had proven that he didn't exterminate easily. Of course if things got too hot, he'd move, but that would not be likely to occur in the immediate future.

The only drawback to the scheme the Ranger contemplated was the necessity of taking part in the outlaw raids; he relied on his wit to stave that off a while.

A peculiarity of Roofless Dobe that would have puzzled the uninitiated was the constant stream of visitors showing up at all hours of the day and night. As a result, anything of interest that happened in the section was quickly learned at Roofless Dobe. So when, a few nights later, the C Bar H lost two hundred head of prime stock and a couple of night hawks who were standing guard in the bargain, Roofless Dobe heard about it before sun-up the next morning.

Jim Hatfield rode off, apparently to work on the southwest pasture, as quickly as possible. As soon as he was off the home range he made a bee-line for the buyer's ranch. He rode swiftly but warily, scanning the trail ahead, watching the sky for the dust cloud kicked up by a fast moving herd. He saw nothing, heard nothing. When he reached the final bend that hid the ranchhouse from view, he slowed Goldy's pace and his vigilance increased.

A single glance told him that the big corral was empty and hadn't been used recently. And when the house came into view he felt that it had a deserted look. No smoke rose from the chimney, the door was closed, the windows blank. To all appearances there was nobody home.

In men who ride with danger as a constant stirrup companion there develops a peculiar sixth sense that warns of peril when none apparently is present. And as he gazed at the ominous looking building, that silent monitor abruptly set up a clamor in a corner of his brain. Tense, alert, he scanned his surroundings. Everything looked peaceful, but the clamor persisted. He slowed Goldy to a walk.

Back of the house a steep, brush-covered slope flung upward to a rounded skyline. His glance raised to the slope, sweeping back and forth.

In a clump of brush a couple of hundred yards up the sag his eye caught a quick sparkle, as of shifted metal gleaming in the sunlight. He hurled himself sideways from the saddle, jerking his Winchester from the boot as he went down. Before he hit the ground a bullet yelled through the space his body had occupied an instant before. From the clump of brush puffed a tell-tale wisp of whitish smoke. He clamped the rifle against his shoulder and sprayed lead into the bush as fast as he could pull the trigger, the reports blending in a drumroll of sound, the ejector lever a blur of movement.

At the fifth shot the bush was violently agitated. Something black pitched from it and went rolling down the slope to come to rest against a boulder.

Hatfield held his fire, his eyes never leaving the brush. But after the echoes of his shots ceased slam-banging back and forth, the silence was unbroken. There was no sign of movement on the slope except a bird that wheeled and fluttered over the bush that had sheltered the drygulcher. Finally it settled into the bush, a pretty good sign that nobody else was holed up there.

Still Hatfield did not move from where he lay in the tall grass and covered by Goldy's shadow. He studied the silent house intently. Nobody appeared, the stillness remained unbroken. He got to his feet, cautiously, his eyes fixed on the crumpled form beside the boulder. Still wary, he climbed the slope, taking advantage of all cover that offered, pausing often to peer and listen, his cocked rifle at the ready. He halted behind a final fringe of growth and again studied the prone drygulcher.

Satisfied that the hellion was really dead

and not playing 'possum, he stepped boldly from the growth. He was not at all surprised to find that the dead man was the lanky buyer with the mis-mated eyes.

"Smart jigger, all right," he remarked aloud, gazing down at the corpse. "That yarn I handed him the other day didn't fool him a bit. He had me sized up for something off-color and I reckon he's been keeping a sharp watch for me ever since. So when he spotted me, he slid out and into the brush. Now the big question is, did he figure things out by himself, or did he meet Morales after I was here and get the lowdown from him. Sure wish I knew the answer to that one.

"The fact that no herd got here makes it look like he did contact Morales. From a description of me, Morales would know who was nosing around. I've a notion that was it, but maybe no."

On the scant chance of finding something of interest, he went through the dead man's pockets, and unearthed nothing of significance. He decided to give the house a once-over.

He approached the building warily; he hadn't forgotten the villainous looking Mexican cook. But he had little fear that he was holed up inside. Had he been there, surely the shooting would have brought him out.

There was nobody in the house and a prolonged search disclosed nothing of significance in the dirty rooms save a large sum of money in a table drawer, which he did not disturb.

He rolled a cigarette and sat down in a rickety chair and pondered the problem of just what was back of the drygulching. If the buyer had just gotten suspicious and decided that he, Hatfield, was a snooper representing either the forces of the law or some rival outfit that hoped to take over his lucrative business, the incident was closed. But if on the other hand he had gotten in touch with Morales and because of what the outlaw told him felt it best to get rid of the Ranger, either because of the urging of Morales or because he felt it was to his own advantage to do so, the matter was far from closed.

That would mean that Morales had been warned that his enemy was on his trail. Which would give him the advantage that Hatfield had hoped to enjoy. He had counted on Morales' assumption that he, as a Ranger, would not follow him beyond the Texas state line, which would perhaps lull the owlhoot into a false sense of security.

He had a feeling that Mary Morales might be right when she said she was convinced that Robert Morales feared him and that that was the chief reason for him pulling out of Texas. And if it were so and Morales learned he was in Arizona he would be on the alert. Morales had spoken true words when he boasted that there was very little law enforcement in this section of Arizona. Not only were the peace officers apparently inclined to be lenient toward organized outlawry, but in addition there was a bitter feud between the two arms of enforcement, one represented by Sheriff Johnny Behan and his county colleagues, the other by the Earps, Virgil and Wyatt, the one Marshal of Tombstone, the other a representative of the Federal Government. Such an overlapping of antagonistic authority did not make for good enforcement.

All of which made it logical to believe that Morales was not particularly concerned over apprehension by local authorities. But if he had learned that Hatfield with a strong personal interest in the matter was close on his heels, he would very likely become much more wary, and Robert Morales on the alert was a problem to tax the capabilities of even the Lone

Wolf. That had already been conclusively proven.

He wondered where the half-breed cook had gotten to. And if he played a more important role in the illegitimate business than appeared on the surface. Perhaps he had but taken the day off, but again perhaps he might have been dispatched with a message to somebody or to make delivery arrangements. Hatfield decided he'd stick around a bit against the chance of his return.

Which brought to mind the body of the drygulcher lying on the slope. Ornery as he had been, it was hardly proper to allow the corpse to be torn by coyotes or vultures. He climbed the slope and carried the body to the ranchhouse, laying it out decently on a couch and covering it with a blanket. He chuckled grimly in anticipation of the Mexican's consternation when he returned and tried to awaken the "sleeping" man.

Hatfield waited until the shadows grew long, and nobody showed up. Finally, thoroughly disgusted, he rode back to the Roofless Dobe. His promising lead had apparently frizzled.

When Hatfield arrived at the ranchhouse, after spending the remaining hours of daylight at chores in the southwest pasture, he found the C Bar H widelooping still a topic of conversation.

"The hands trailed the critters into Mexico and lost 'em in the canyons down there," said Joe Hill. "Those oilers are getting too darn smart. I tell you something's got to be done about it. We're losing money right and left because of 'em. I'd had my eye on those C Bar H cows for a week. I tell you it ain't right."

Others nodded emphatic agreement. The Mexicans were doin' them wrong! Hatfield forgot some of his own irritation in amusement at this outburst of righteous indignation. Even the grim business of outlawry had its lighter moments.

He wondered if Joe Hill might be right about the latest depredation being the work of raiders from south of the Border. If Morales did the chore, he evidently had another market someplace. That would be like him, all right. He trusted nobody and perhaps he was suspicious of the buyer with the mis-mated eyes. Which was not unlikely. Such men were to be trusted just as far as it was to their self-interest to be trustworthy.

"And that particular specimen looked like he'd sell his own grandfather for what his hide and tallow would bring," he told himself.

15

Joe Hill as in a restless mood, doubtless induced by his excitement over the C Bar H widelooping.

"How about a little ride over to Paradise?" he suggested. "Payday at the mines and the smelters and it had ought to be lively."

However, nobody appeared to be interested.

"Not in the notion tonight," said Hicks. "Maybe Charley will go with you." But Charley also shook his head.

Hill turned to Hatfield. "How about you, Jim?" he asked. "Reckon you haven't ever been to Paradise; want to come along?"

Hatfield decided to go, on the faint chance that Morales might drop in for the payday jamboree and perhaps to get a line on some easy pickings.

"All right," he told Hill, "if it's okay by the Boss."

"Go right ahead and have a good time," said Hicks. "Don't be in a hurry to get back; you've earned a mite of diversion. But don't let that card shark get you into a poker game or you're liable to come back without your pants. Every time I play with him I ain't the same for a week."

Hatfield and Hill saddled up and left Roofless Dobe shortly after sundown. They took it easy and it was well past full dark when they arrived at the mining town. Hitching their horses at a convenient rack they crossed the dusty street to a big and well-lighted saloon with an exceptionally high and wide door.

They had a drink, then Hill wandered over to the dance floor and found a good looking partner. Hatfield remained at the bar, surveying the crowd with interest.

Paradise was booming and the miners and others had apparently come to the conclusion that money was something liable to burn holes in a man's pockets. Against such a calamity, they were proceeding to get rid of it with dispatch. The bar was packed, all the games were filled, the dance floor crowded. Hatfield studied faces intently. If Morales should happen to drop in there was no telling what his appearance at the moment might be like. Hatfield was pretty sure, however, that he couldn't mistake the outlaw's glittering eyes. They were a better brand mark of Robert Morales, he thought, than his golden hair or even his sardonic *"Buenos noches, Senor!"*

Suddenly his gaze fixed on the profile of a man sitting in a faro game not far from the door. It wasn't Morales, of that Hatfield was certain, but that profile had a vaguely familiar look. Where had he lately seen that high cheek bone, that flat fleshy nose, and that heavy, underslung jaw? The man turned a bit and Hatfield recognized the drygulching cattle buyer's half-breed cook.

Looked like the fellow was just out for a day's entertainment; then he noted that the cook kept shooting glances toward the door, as if expecting somebody.

Getting more interested in the fellow, Hatfield left the bar and sauntered around the room, finally dropping into a chair close to the faro game and almost directly behind the cook's seat. He rolled a cigarette and awaited developments, if any. The cook kept shooting expectant glances toward the door.

Finally, it appeared that his vigil was rewarded. A man who looked like a Mexican came in, glanced about and made his way to the faro table. He and the cook conversed for a moment in low tones. Hatfield could only catch an occasional word of Spanish — *ganado* (cattle), *esta noche* (tonight), *pronto* (at once — hurry).

A final inaudible mutter, the cook nodded, the other turned and left the room. A moment later the cook cashed in his chips and also left. Hatfield got up and sauntered after him. He caught Joe Hill's eye as he passed the dance floor and called to him,

"Going out for a bit of fresh air; see you later."

Hill waved his hand and went on dancing.

When Hatfield reached the street the cook was just across at the rack and in the act of unhitching a very good looking bay horse. He mounted and rode up the street. As soon as he turned the corner, Hatfield forked Goldy and rode after him. As he turned the corner, he caught a glimpse of his quarry just rounding another. Hatfield followed. His curiosity was aroused. Something concerning cattle was going on tonight. He deduced that from the fragments of conversation he had overheard.

Where the street turned into a trail that ran south by west across the valley, he caught sight of the cook again, riding at a good pace. Hatfield proceeded to do as expert a job of tailing as he was able.

But the cook apparently knew just where he was going and wasn't concerned about anybody on his track. He never looked around.

After an hour or so of riding, Hatfield decided that the breed was undoubtedly heading for the dead buyer's ranchhouse, Things were getting more interesting. The breed had gotten a message that had to do with cattle. He certainly had not gotten it from the buyer. Hatfield had left *him* some hours before, in no condition to send messages. It wasn't hard to deduce that the message had in all probability been from somebody contemplating running a herd to the buyer. And there was a chance that the somebody might be Morales. Perhaps he had holed up the herd he stole from the C Bar H in some hidden canyon till things cooled down a bit. Not at all illogical to think he would have, with the C Bar H cowhand swallerforkin' all over the valley. This might be the break Hatfield had hoped for.

Hatfield dropped back a bit as they neared the ranchhouse, but when the breed passed out of sight around the last bend, he quickened Goldy's pace. He rounded the turn just in time to see a light flash up in the ranchhouse. He backed Goldy into a thicket beside the trail and waited.

For several minutes the house was silent. Then he heard a pound of feet on the bare boards. The door flung open and the breed rushed out. Without closing the door he mounted his horse and sent him tearing back the way he had come. Hatfield waited a moment after he passed the thicket, then set out in pursuit.

But this time he was quickly spotted. The breed kept glancing over his shoulder, as if some grisly horror rode behind. He quickened his horse's gait. It was a good animal but Goldy had no trouble keeping pace.

Hatfield did not try to close the distance. He loosened his rifle in the saddle boot against eventualities, but made no attempt to use it. He was chiefly interested in learning where the fellow was bound for.

For several miles the race continued, the breed constantly glancing back. He whisked around a turn formed by a jut of cliff and Hatfield sent Goldy flashing after him. The sorrel whisked around the bend and head-on into the lead steers of a sizable herd traveling in the opposite direction. Goldy was almost knocked off his feet. The cows began scattering in fright.

From behind the herd a gun cracked, again and again. Lead whistled past Hatfield. Somebody was blazing away as fast as he could pull the trigger. Both Hatfield's guns let go with a rattling crash, though there was nothing but an elusive shadow to shoot at. The bellowing of the terrified cattle added to the uproar.

Suddenly the shadowy gun wielder whirled his horse and streaked off down the trail. Hatfield could see that he was a tall man and splendidly mounted, and that was about all. But there was no doubt in his mind as to who it was. He shouted to Goldy, but the sorrel was hopelessly entangled in the milling herd. By the time he managed to win free, the fugitive was nowhere in sight and in the gloom it was impossible to tell which way he might have turned.

Hatfield pulled the sorrel to a halt and examined him to make sure he had taken no serious injury. Then he went in search of the breed. The fellow might be induced to answer a few questions, if he could find him.

He found him, all right, but the breed wasn't talking. He had a blue bullet hole between his eyes. Hatfield muttered an all-embracing curse on the positively infernal way in which Morales always managed to get the best of any situation, and he proceeded to round up the scattered herd. He noted with little satisfaction that the cows bore the C Bar H brand.

16

Curly Bill held court in Galeyville, where he reigned supreme, surrounded by his loyal retainers; but not without certain defections of loyalty, as Jim Hatfield was to learn the day he rode into Galeyville.

Hatfield knew that Brocius hung out in Babcock's, so he stabled his horse and proceeded there on foot. He found Brocius at the bar drinking and talking with Jim Wallace, one of his men. Hatfield thought he looked in an irritable mood.

He greeted Hatfield heartily, however, bought him a drink and then said,

"Go over to the table by the door and sit with John Ringo. I'll be with you in a minute."

Hatfield went over to the table, where Ringo gave him a courteous greeting and made room for him. Curly Bill remained at the bar, talking with Wallace. The talk appeared to be approaching the proportions of an argument. Wallace was a tough hombre, vicious, bad tempered, and when drinking he was apt to be quarrelsome. Things that Hatfield learned later, although he guessed as much after a look at Wallace.

Ringo was telling the others about some recent experience in Tombstone. Hatfield listened, but his attention was mostly fixed on the altercation going on at the bar. Curly Bill's voice was growing louder as he downed more whiskey. Suddenly he lashed out and knocked Wallace crashing to the floor.

Wallace, a lean, slender man, rose to his feet slowly, blood on his face. He doubtless realized that he was no match for the burly Brocius with his fists. He wiped the blood from his mouth with the back of his hand.

"I'll be waiting for you outside," he said thickly and walked from the saloon.

Curly Bill was too befuddled with drink to immediately understand what Wallace meant. Then it sank in and with a roar of anger he rushed to the door.

Jim Hatfield, seeing Brocius was half drunk and that real trouble was building up, reached the street almost as quickly as the outlaw chief.

Wallace was standing behind his horse at the curb, his gun trained across the saddle. He fired the instant Brocius appeared and shot him through the cheek. Curly Bill staggered back and Wallace took deliberate aim at the reeling man.

Jim Hatfield drew and shot with a flicker of movement too swift for the eye to follow. Wallace's leveled Colt spun from his hand and thudded on the ground. He wrung his blood-dripping fingers and yelled with pain.

The crowd was streaming from the saloon. Hatfield regarded them with icy gray eyes. For the moment he forgot the role he was playing. He was the peace officer ready to enforce law and order, through the smoke of his gun, if necessary.

However, the situation was quickly under control. Constable Jerry Barton ran up, grabbed Wallace and placed him under arrest. The crowd milled about. "Get a rope!" somebody yelled. But a few words from John Ringo quieted the crowd and they streamed back into the saloon. Wallace was hustled off to the lockup for safe keeping till things cooled down.

Curly Bill, considerably sobered, was

swabbing the blood from his bullet gashed cheek. He regarded Hatfield strangely.

"Feller," he said, "I'll never forget what you did for me today. If it hadn't been for you, right now, I reckon I'd be wherever my sort finally goes. No, I'll not forget it, and if you ever want a favor from Bill Brocius, no matter how little, no matter how big, just ask and don't waste any time waiting to ask. Think I'll go to the back room and lie down a bit. My teeth hurt."

"I'll go with you and tie up your face," offered Ringo. "See you in a little, Hatfield."

They headed for the back room. Hatfield went back to his table, the eye of every man in the place on him.

In the back room, Ringo remarked, "Remember what I said about him over at the ranch? I was right. I never saw such a draw in my life. Fact is, I *didn't* see it. That gun just appeared in his hand. And he drew and shot inside the time it took Wallace to pull trigger twice, and that gun smoked the instant it cleared leather. He's the kind of a gun slinger that happens once in a lifetime. He'd make Buckskin Frank Leslie or Doc Holliday look like a sick snail climbing a slick log."

"Don't say things like that!" complained

Curly Bill. "But you're right, he's a whizzer. We can use him."

"Yes, but I don't think we'll get the chance, Bill; he wouldn't fit into our bunch."

"Why?"

Ringo's voice was suddenly surcharged with bitterness. "Because he's what I always wanted to be and never was — a *man!*"

However, less discerning outlaws gave Hatfield a royal welcome when he returned to the table and evidently accepted him as one of themselves, freely discussing past and future exploits in his presence.

Hatfield knew that while somewhat dubious as to source, he was being paid a high compliment. These bold, reckless men had respect for courage and ability; their praise was sincere.

In the back room, Curly Bill, his jaw bandaged and a cigarette between his lips, was feeling better. He brought up the subject of Jim Hatfield again.

"If he ain't outside the law, John, what do you think he's doing here?" he asked.

"I think," said Ringo slowly, "that he's looking for somebody. I watched his eyes when I was with him at the table. They gave every man in the room a careful once-over, and anybody coming in the door got the same thing. He seemed to be always watching for a face."

"I wouldn't want to have him looking for me. Think he's a sheriff or something?"

"Could be," admitted Ringo, "but then again it could be a personal matter. He's from Texas, all right, and we Texans are long on blood feuds. That's what got me started on the wrong track, you know. I killed the three men who murdered my brother."

"If we knew who he's looking for we'd help find the hellion," Curly Bill instantly declared. "Hope it's Wyatt Earp."

"Not likely," Ringo replied with a laugh. "Wyatt's well known and he isn't doing any hiding. But I'd back Hatfield against even Wyatt Earp."

"I'd like to back *him* into a hole in the ground," growled Brocius, apropos the famous frontier marshal for whom he had no love. "Sound Hatfield out a bit, John, and try and find out who he *is* after. Nobody can come into the section without us learning about it sooner or later, and I'd like to do him a favor; I owe him plenty. By the way, Milt Hicks thinks it was Hatfield held up the Benson stage."

"I know," replied Ringo. "Milt is always

putting two and two together and making five. I don't believe it."

Meanwhile, ignorant of the formidable forces rallying to his support, Jim Hatfield was listening idly to a story told by Billy Claibourne who had just come in dusty and thirsty from a long ride.

"I've seen some queer things in this loco tail-end of creation," Claibourne said, "but today I figure I saw the queerest one of 'em all. I was riding from Tucson to Tombstone on the Tucson road. You know where the road runs into that big notch about fifteen miles out of Tucson, with slopes all growed with brush shooting up on both sides? Well, I'd come to the notch and I rode up into the brush a little ways to 'tend to some personal business. I was out of sight from the road and so was my horse. Well, I heard a horse coming from toward Tombstone. I peeked through the brush and saw a feller riding into the notch. He was a big tall feller with yellow hair. I thought at first it was John Ringo, but it wasn't."

Hatfield abruptly became all attention and very interested indeed in what else Claibourne had to say.

"Well," said Billy, after taking a drink, "I watched that feller come along. He'd slowed up and was walking his horse and looking to right and left as if he was hunting something. Sort of got me curious, the way he was acting, so I stayed put.

"Almost opposite to where I was hunkered down in the brush, he pulled up and unforked. He stood there for a minute still looking around. Then he started walking back and forth along the road, slow, like he was pacing off distances, and still peeking and peering at the brush on either side. He walked up to a tree that grew right at the edge of the road and looked it over like he'd never seen such a thing before. He walked around the tree, got behind it and sort of squinted at the road, like he was taking a sight at something. Then he pulled out a knife and began cutting a deep gash in the trunk of the tree.

"After a while, he finished cutting and went back to the road, still looking around. He spotted a couple more trees on the other side of the road, almost opposite the first one. He looked them over, got behind them and squinted. Then he went to work and cut gashes in them, too. Then he put his knife up, looked all around again, forked his cayuse and rode back the way he'd come, toward Tombstone. I figured he was plumb loco and might do anything, so I stayed right where I was till he was out of sight. Then I rode down out of the brush and headed for Tombstone. Didn't see hide or hair of him again, and I didn't want to. Feller sort of give me the creeps the way he was acting."

His hearers received the yarn with a certain amount of incredulity.

"Sure you didn't stay in Snake-hooch Joe's place too long in Tucson?" one asked. "That tarantuler juice Snake-hooch serves is liable to make a feller see most anything."

"I was plumb sober," Claibourne declared. "Was 'long about the middle of the morning."

"You must have rid mighty fast to get to Tombstone and back here by now," observed another critic.

"Didn't get to Tombstone," Claibourne explained. "Maybe it was because I was thinking about that loco gent so much, but I decided I didn't want to go to Tombstone. I turned off and came on here."

The others laughed and the matter was dropped.

Jim Hatfield sat silent, his black brows drawing together, a sure sign the Lone Wolf was doing some hard thinking. He couldn't make head or tail of Claibourne's reminiscence, but from his description, he felt pretty sure that Claibourne had seen Robert Morales and that Morales was up to something that would bear looking into.

"I've never been to Tucson," he observed to his neighbor. "Stage run there?"

"Uh-huh, between Tombstone and Tucson," the other replied. "Tucson is on the railroad and the stage brings the mail to Tombstone where there ain't none. Leaves early in the morning from both places. You can ride there from here, through Silver Creek Canyon and cutting across the valley. Not a bad ride."

A few minutes later Hatfield left the table and sauntered to the back room, where he found Curly Bill and Ringo still talking and smoking.

"Mr. Brocius," he said, "I believe you said it would be all right for me to ask you a favor?"

"Ask it," Curly Bill instantly replied.

"Well," said Hatfield, "I'd like a few days off from the job."

"A few days!" snorted Brocius. "Take a week — take a month! Your pay'll go right on and the job'll be waiting for you when you come back."

"Much obliged," Hatfield said and left the room.

"Don't forget, the job'll be there when

you come back," Curly Bill called after him.

"Yes, if he comes back," Ringo remarked as the door closed.

"What do you mean by that?" asked Curly Bill.

"I mean that I'm doubtful that he'll come back," said the shrewd Ringo. "I've a notion he heard something in the other room. I'm going to try and find out what the boys at that table were talking about."

It didn't take Ringo long to get Billy Claibourne to repeat the story of his adventure on the Tucson road. He lingered a few minutes after Claibourne finished his tale and then went back to Brocius.

"Bill," he said, "remember that jigger with the yellow hair you saw shoot Cal Houck? Bill, I believe that's the man Hatfield is looking for."

"How'd you find that out?" asked Brocius.

"Guesswork," Ringo answered. "Guesswork and putting two and two together and making four instead of five. Bill, I think I'll ride to Tombstone tomorrow."

"Okay," acceded Brocius, "but for Pete's sake don't get into a row with the Earps! And drop in and see Sheriff Behan; he's our friend."

The ride to Tucson was a long one. Hatfield got there several hours after sunrise. He had no trouble locating the stage station.

"Stage for Tombstone?" an attendant answered his query. "Left better than two hours ago. You can get another one this afternoon."

Hatfield thanked his informant and rode southeast on the road from Tucson to Tombstone. He suffered a disquieting foreboding that he was too late to prevent whatever Morales had in mind, but thought his best bet was to follow the stage on the faint chance of getting in on anything that might happen.

Plenty happened on the Tucson road, none of it satisfactory from a peace officer's point of view.

To reach the notch where Billy Claibourne witnessed the yellow-haired man's peculiar and mysterious actions, the road writhed up a long and steep slope. By the time the stage reached the crest where the notch began, the horses were breathing hard and sweating. They topped the sag at a slow walk and the driver allowed them to continue to walk through the shadowy notch between its brush grown encroaching slopes.

Beside the guard sat a Wells Fargo Express Company messenger, a shotgun across his knees; one always accompanied the stage. However, neither guard nor driver were more than ordinarily on the alert, for the stage was carrying nothing but mail this trip, no express, no passengers, and the mail held little inducement for the outlaw fraternity. So both driver and messenger were unprepared and astonished when, about half way through the notch, a voice rang out from the brush in the conventional,

"Hands up!"

The driver instinctively jerked his horses to a halt. The messenger clutched at his shotgun, then let go of it in a hurry.

He was staring into the muzzles of three rifle barrels protruding from behind trees that edged the road. His hands went up; the driver's were already there.

The growth rustled and a tall, yellow-haired man rode into view. He had glittering black eyes, and two heavy guns swinging at his hips.

"All right, boys," he called. "Hold on 'em, and if they make a move, let 'em have it. Stay right like you are, gents, and you won't get hurt," he told the driver and messenger.

199

He dismounted in leisurely fashion and walked to the coach. He flung open the door, stepped inside and began rummaging about amid the big heap of mail sacks. For several minutes he pulled and hauled, while the two gentlemen on the high seat above sat rigid, their aching arms above their heads, staring fearfully at the black rifle muzzles.

"The hellion knew just what he wanted and kept on hunting till he found it," the driver said later.

The bandit reappeared bearing a small locked pouch. He tucked it under his arm, mounted his horse and drew a gun with a swift, easy movement.

"All right," he said, gesturing with the big Colt, "turn that shebang and head back the way you come. Better not look behind you till you're on the sag on the other side. The boys have itchy trigger fingers and those saddle guns carry a long ways."

The driver obeyed without argument and sent the stage back down the trail considerably faster than it had come up. He and the messenger sat with stiff necks till they were well down the far slope.

"Now what the devil did the sidewinder want with that mail pouch?" the driver demanded as he whipped up his horses.

He found out later, from the wrathful station agent. The pouch which had been surreptitiously hidden among the mail sacks under the mistaken notion that it would not be noticed and no suspicion aroused that the stage carried anything of value, had contained quite a few thousand dollars worth of diamonds and other gems consigned to a Tombstone jeweler.

"But how did that sidewinder know it was there?" demanded the driver.

"How do those brush-popping devils know everything that's going on?" countered the agent. "I told Burton it was a fool idea, but he wouldn't listen."

Jim Hatfield was about five miles out of Tucson when he heard the rumble of the returning stage. He pulled aside to let it pass. Around the bend it careened, the driver bellowing at his lathered horses.

"What's the matter?" Hatfield shouted as the stage whizzed past.

"Robbers!" yelled the messenger, waving his shotgun. "The woods are full of them!"

The stage rocked on down the trail in a cloud of dust. Hatfield gazed after it a moment, then rode on at a moderate pace. No use to hurry, he was still ten miles from the notch. But he hoped to learn how Morales pulled it.

When he entered the notch, Hatfield was very much on the alert, studying the growth on either side, watching the trail ahead. Suddenly he jerked Goldy to a halt. He was gazing into the muzzles of three rifles protruding from behind tree trunks. He sat perfectly still, not moving his hands. To do otherwise was tantamount to committing suicide, or so it appeared.

But no peremptory command rang out from the brush. The black muzzles yawned at him in unbroken silence. Abruptly he understood. Muttering an oath he swung down from the saddle and walked to the nearest tree. The black pupil of the muzzle eyed him ominously but never wavered. He paused to stare at the contraption.

The rifle was skillfully lashed into the gash Morales had cut, so as to give the impression that it was held by a man concealed behind the tree trunk. The same obtained with the other two.

"A trap to catch fools like that driver — and myself!" he growled. "Well, this is a new one. Wonder how many more tricks that hellion has in his poke."

Too disgusted to even touch the things he returned to Goldy.

"Let some other chuckle-head get a scare and take them down," he grunted as he mounted and headed for Tombstone, letting his tired horse choose his own gait. Still no sense in hurrying. Morales had scored again!

When he reached Tombstone he was deathly weary. He stabled his horse, rented a room at the Russ House and went to bed. He slept until later afternoon and then sallied forth in search of food and possible information. The first he expected to find, about the second he was decidedly dubious.

Hatfield had visited Tombstone some years before and was fairly familiar with the Silver City; but he marveled at the changes a comparatively short period had wrought.

Tombstone was at the height of its opulence, the largest settlement in Arizona. Nobody dreamed that a year later it would be little more than a ghost town, never to regain its predominant position in Arizona affairs.

There was at the moment nothing to predict such a disastrous miracle for the roaring boom town, the most picturesque, fantastic, and richest mining settlement America ever knew, perhaps.

It was a mining town in the heart of what had always been and still was cattle country. Cowboys in chaps, spurs and broadbrimmed Stetsons rode its streets and rubbed shoulders with miners in blue woolen shirts and silver millionaires in silk and broadcloth.

Tombstone was the strangest mixture of sedate wealth and thundering violence that could be imagined. Gunmen fought it out in the streets, while sober citizens went to church. There were pink teas and cultured conversation while around the corner was a garish dance hall. The sheriff hauled in a miscreant while desperadoes just outside town held up the stage. Bad men and preachers passed on the street with friendly nods. Mine owners sat across the table from waxen-faced, steelnerved card sharps and matched wits with them over the pasteboards, and often came out ahead. Some of them had themselves been dealers before Ed Schieffelin scratched the bleak, unprofitable appearing hills to the north with his pick and found them bursting with silver. Outlaws from a score of other camps came to town and found fat pickings. Tombstone boasted the finest saloons west of Chicago.

While dignified lawyers argued briefs

in the courthouse, more business for them was in the making just outside the doors. An ambitious speculator built a grandstand so that citizens could view a multiple hanging in comfort, at $2.50 a head. Other citizens tore it down as an affront to the town's dignity. Meanwhile, citizens of neighboring Bisbee, where the murders for which the court at Tombstone had ordered the five killers to pay the supreme penalty occurred, decided that justice in Tombstone moved with creaking wheels. They came to Tombstone and took one miscreant out of jail and hanged him on their own account. A coroner's jury ponderously decided that the gentleman in question, one Jim Heath, came to his untimely end "due to strangulation, self-inflicted or otherwise." Which satisfied everybody except, perhaps, Jim Heath. Tombstone was quite a town.

Hatfield walked along Fifth Street from Toughnut and turned into Allen Street, the town's main thoroughfare. He entered the Oriental bar, resplendent with oil paintings, plateglass mirrors, brass and mahogany, all housed in a clapboard building that was little more than a shack. He found a table, sat down and glanced around with interest.

At the far end of the bar stood a tall blond, lion-like man with cold gray eyes and a drooping mustache. He recognized the famous Wyatt Earp, Deputy United States Marshal and owner of the Oriental. Nearby lounged saturnine, cadaverous Doc Holliday, the trigger-man of the Earp faction, immaculately attired in gray but with a sawed-off shotgun strapped to his side under his faultlessly fitting coat. There were three bartenders on duty, one of them quiet, gentlemanly Buckskin Frank Leslie, as courteous a desperado as ever shot an enemy in the back.

Hatfield knew that Earp and Holliday were studying him as he ordered a meal and ate unconcernedly, wondering who he was and where he came from. Their interest quickened a little later when a tall, yellow-haired man walked in. It was John Ringo. He nodded to them and, not to be outdone in politeness, they nodded back, albeit a bit stiffly.

Ringo spotted Hatfield and strolled over to his table. He dropped into a chair and eyed the Ranger for a moment.

"How are you, Hatfield?" he asked. "Did you catch him?"

Hatfield dissembled his surprise, his face

emotionless. "Nope," he replied. "Why do you ask that?"

"Guesswork," said Ringo. "Guesswork and putting two and two together. Understand the Tucson stage was held up this morning."

"Understand it was," Hatfield agreed.

"I heard how it was pulled," said Ringo, laughing a little. "A cute trick. Guess that yellow-haired gent Billy Claibourne saw fooling around in the notch yesterday was setting the stage."

"Guess he was," Hatfield nodded.

"And he's the jigger you're after," Ringo stated conclusively. "Well, Hatfield, I'm here to help you get a line on that fellow. I know this town like the palm of my hand and everybody in it. If he came on to Tombstone, as very likely he did, the chances are I can find somebody who has seen him here. I gather he's the sort that attracts notice, according to Bill's description of him."

Hatfield nodded and was silent for a moment. He did not discount the value of this unexpected offer of assistance. As Ringo said, he knew everybody, and if Morales had really come to Tombstone, the outlaw would doubtless be able to learn of it and his possible whereabouts.

"Thanks, John," he accepted the offer. "I appreciate it."

"Think nothing of it," said Ringo. "You saved Bill's life and I reckon Bill Brocius is the only real friend I have in the world. Let's go."

17

They left the Oriental, the curious glances of Holliday and Wyatt Earp following them, and proceeded to visit place after place. They dropped in at the famous Crystal Palace on the northwest corner of Fifth and Allen Streets, a gray frame building with overhanging eaves that protected patrons from the summer sun, where Hatfield met fussy, alert Sheriff Johnny Behan and his handsome young chief deputy, Billy Breckenridge. They gave the famous Can Can Restaurant a once-over. It was not until dusk was falling that they hit paydirt.

"Yes, John, I remember a fellow who looked like what you say," a bartender told them. "He came in around noon and had a drink. Hitched his horse outside and it looked like he'd been doing considerable riding. He went across the street to the bank."

"Wonder what the hell he wanted there?" muttered Ringo. "The bank wasn't held up today that I've heard of. Come on, Hatfield, we'll go over there. It's closed but the chances are Dave Whelan the cashier will be working late — he usually is the first of the week — and he'll let us in."

They crossed to the bank. A light was burning in the office and they knocked on the door. A moment later a man peered through a peephole. There was a sound of bars being removed and the door swung open to reveal an elderly man wearing glasses.

"Hello, John," he greeted. "Come to stick us up?"

"Not today, Dave," replied Ringo. "I got a few pesos. Some other time perhaps. Dave, I want you to know Jim Hatfield, a friend of mine, but not my sort. Hatfield, this is Dave Whelan."

Hatfield shook hands with the cashier who gave him a keen but not unfriendly look.

"What can I do for you gentlemen?" he asked.

"Dave," said Ringo, "did a tall fellow with yellow hair, I'd judge about the color of mine, and bad eyes come in around noon?"

The cashier nodded. "I remember him," he said. "A well spoken young fellow. He changed gold for paper money, big bills. A lot of money. I wondered where he got such a large amount, but it was none of my business and I had a feeling that he was a kind that might resent questions."

"The chances are he would have, in a way you wouldn't have liked," Ringo agreed dryly. "Did you notice which way he went when he left here?"

"Yes," answered the cashier. "He sort of aroused my curiosity and I watched through the window as he rode off. I'd say he was heading for the Old Spanish Trail. Friend of yours, John?"

Ringo shook his head. "Hatfield would like to have a little talk with him," he explained.

Whelan regarded the Ranger shrewdly but asked no questions. Only he remarked as he closed the door, "Glad to have met you, Mr. Hatfield. Good hunting!"

Outside the bank, Ringo paused. "Well, what do you think?" he asked.

"I think," Hatfield replied quietly, "that he's leaving the section. That's why he changed heavy gold for bills that are easy to pack."

"My sentiments," agreed Ringo. "What

are you going to do?"

"I'm leaving you now, John," Hatfield replied. "I'm going to get my horse. Thanks again for everything. Hope I'll see you again sometime."

"I doubt it," Ringo answered somberly. "I've a feeling I haven't got much more time. Not that I give a hoot, for I tell you I've had enough of the world and life. So long, Hatfield, and as Dave said, good hunting!"

He shook hands and crossed the street to the saloon. Hatfield watched his tall form outlined for an instant against the light. Then he turned and headed for the stable where he left Goldy.

After saddling up, he paused at a general store and bought some staple provisions which he stowed in his saddle pouches. After which he rode out of Tombstone and turned east on the Old Spanish Trail that ran from California to San Antonio and beyond.

Until past midnight he rode on under the glittering stars. He made camp beside a little stream and slept for a few hours, rising before dawn to cook some breakfast before he continued the pursuit. He was banking on the assumption that Morales would not ride swiftly, having no reason to believe he was pursued. Around nine o'clock he came to a little crossroads inn that catered to cowhands and prospectors. He paused for a cup of coffee and to ask a few questions.

"Yes, a feller like you describe stayed here last night," said the innkeeper. "He rode on a couple of hours back."

Hatfield thanked his host and sent Goldy eastward at a fast pace, scanning the trail ahead, alert and watchful at every bend and the crest of each rise. It was getting along toward evening when he spotted his quarry. He had topped a sag and there on the downward slope was a single horseman, something more than a mile distant. Hatfield's heart leaped exultantly. The distance was too great to distinguish features, but he was confident that the lone rider was Morales. He sent Goldy down the slope at a fast pace.

Hunted men look behind them. Hatfield saw the rider turn in his saddle. He seemed to be studying him. It was highly doubtful that Morales would recognize him at that distance, but apparently the outlaw wanted no part of this stranger riding hard on his trail. He quickened his horse's gait, glancing back from time to time.

Although the quarry had a good start, Hatfield was confident of the final result. Morales was superbly mounted, no doubt as to that, but Hatfield was convinced that his horse, no matter how good it was, was no match for Goldy in a gruelling chase. Hatfield settled himself in the saddle and spoke encouraging words to the great sorrel who was steadily lengthening his stride.

Slowly but surely Goldy closed the distance. The near mile and a half shrank to a mile, shrank still more as the gray trail flowed under the flying sorrel's irons.

The trail ran across level prairie, but some distance ahead were low hills. And flowing from a cut to the west were the twin steel ribbons of a railroad that the trail crossed.

There was no doubt in Hatfield's mind now but that the man ahead was Morales. There was no mistaking that easy graceful posture. And once the sunlight gleamed on his golden hair.

Morales had almost reached the crossing when out of the cut boomed a long freight train. Hatfield saw him pull to a halt; he was blocked!

But even as Hatfield reached down to loosen his Winchester in the saddle boot,

Morales whirled his horse and sent it racing alongside the swiftly moving train. Hatfield saw him lean far over and grip a grabiron on the side of a swaying boxcar. He was instantly jerked from the hull and for a moment dangled by one hand. Then his feet got a purchase on a lower iron. He waved a derisive hand at his pursuer. When the foaming sorrel reached the crossing, the red caboose of the freight train was bobbing away in the distance.

Hatfield pulled Goldy to a halt, fished the makin's from his pocket and rolled a cigarette. No sense in trying to match horse flesh against steel and steam. Through the blue haze of the smoke he considered the situation. Morales would doubtless ride to the next stop, wherever that was, buy another horse and proceed with a comfortable lead on his pursuer.

But Hatfield wasn't finished yet; he had an ace in the hole. He believed he knew what Morales was headed for, and if so, he still had a long ways to go. And there was always the chance of overtaking him on the trail. Unless he had the unusual luck to obtain a really excellent mount, Goldy was an asset not to overlook.

Hatfield still felt fairly optimistic. He dismounted and gave the sorrel a good rubdown. Then, after allowing him a breather he rode on, knowing that later the trail would parallel the railroad for many miles.

Hatfield slept out again that night, making a comfortable camp where a spring bubbled from beneath an overhanging cliff. He moved on at sun-up, riding at a moderate pace for he knew the chase would be a long one. He passed several small settlements, little more than a scattering of cabins around a huge watertank. He felt confident that Morales would not have left the train at such spots, for they provided no opportunity of obtaining a horse. All of which, however, was in Morales' favor. He was steadily increasing his lead.

The Ranger noticed one fact, however, that might be in his favor. At each watering point was a long siding, now empty. It was likely the freight would pause there to pick up loads or empties, also to allow passenger trains or westbound freights to pass, which meant delay. Still doubtful as to the ultimate result, he rode on.

Late evening of the second day he reached a larger village built on both sides of the railroad. It boasted cattle corrals and loading pens, a livery stable, a restaurant and a general store. Hatfield paused first at the stable which was kept by a surly individual with a very questioning eye. Back of the stable was a small corral in which grazed several horses. This looked promising.

"Didn't happen to sell a horse to a tall, yellow-haired gent with black eyes, the past day or two?" he asked.

"And what if I did?" the keeper asked suspiciously.

Hatfield drew his Ranger badge from its cunningly concealed secret pocket in his broad leather belt. He knew he was well into New Mexico now, and not far from the Texas state line. Ranger authority would be respected here. He held the famous silver star set on a silver circle before the stablekeeper's eyes.

The man instantly became voluble. "Sure I sold one," he said. "Fellow must have gotten off the eastbound freight. He paid cash and I didn't see why I should ask any questions. He slept here and then rode on east early this morning. Did the feller do something wrong?"

"Considerable," Hatfield replied, "but you didn't do anything wrong in selling him the horse, so don't worry. Was it a good horse?"

"Not bad," said the stablekeeper, looking much relieved. "Nothing like that critter of yours, but a pretty good cayuse. He picked out the best of the lot."

Hatfield nodded. "I hanker for a surrounding and a place to pound my ear tonight," he said.

"Good eating house right down the tracks," said the stable keeper. "The railroad boys and the cowhands use it. And I got a couple of rooms above the stalls if you'd like to sleep close to your horse. Clean and no bugs."

18

Hatfield ate a good meal and slept in a comfortable bed. When daylight came he took to the road again. He was in a more cheerful frame of mind. Morales' lead was less than he had expected, and if he was riding a mediocre horse, there was still a chance of overtaking him on the main trail.

But the going was rough and progress slow. The next day was pretty well advanced when Hatfield knew he was back on Texas soil. And the trail was edging toward the Rio Grande. If his theory was right, Morales would be leaving it before long and following him in the trackless waste to the south would be a well nigh hopeless task. He pushed Goldy as hard as he dared and kept a constant watch ahead. In late afternoon he once more caught a glimpse of his quarry.

He had topped a tall ridge beyond the opposite slope of which lay a wide valley. On the far side of the valley was another ridge up which the trail climbed. And on the crest a moving dot that he knew to be a horseman was outlined against the sky for a moment. Then the rider vanished down the opposite sag.

Hatfield knew that it was very probable that the fugitive had seen *him* outlined against the sky brightened by the westing sun. He spoke to Goldy and the gallant sorrel quickened his pace. Half an hour later he crested the opposite ridge.

Down a steep sag the trail flowed, winding like a hurrying snake. Down to a level expanse across a couple of miles of which Hatfield could make out the dobes and shacks of a small river village. A couple of miles from the village, to the east, was the bulk of a large white ranch-house, doubtless the residence of the owner of the cattle land on which the villagers found employment. Of Morales there was no sign. Very likely he had already passed through the village.

Some miles to the south, Hatfield saw an irregular silvery flash that he knew must be the Rio Grande. He rode on eagerly. There was a chance that the outlaw had not seen him top the ridge west of the valley, and he might pause at the village for food and rest. Hatfield warily approached the cluster of buildings, ready for instant action. He rode past the scattered outlying homes and into the public square.

A number of people were gathered there. A shout went up at his appearance and the Ranger found himself looking into the muzzles of a score of rifles pointing from every direction. He jerked Goldy to a halt and raised his hands.

"What's the big notion?" he called, and repeated the words in Spanish.

A babble of voices answered as the crowd closed in on him. Hatfield understood Spanish but he couldn't make head or tail of the screeching pandemonium.

He caught the words, *"Ajo!"* — halt — *"Ladrone!"* — thief, and a few more that appeared to indicate he was looked upon with a very unfavorable light. Resistance was useless and he permitted himself to be hauled from the saddle and stripped of his guns. The more he tried to explain, the greater grew the confusion, the excited *peons* all yelling at once. Hands seized him and he was hustled to a stout, log calaboose, thrust into the filthy interior and the door clanged shut behind him.

The room, which boasted a single barred window, was devoid of furnishings save for a blanketless bunk of rough boards built against a wall. Hatfield sat down on the bunk, fished out the makin's and rolled a cigarette. What it was all about he hadn't the slightest notion, but one thing was painfully apparent: Robert Morales had put over another of his smooth tricks. He doubtless had passed through the pueblo and had contrived to arouse the ignorant villagers against his pursuer.

Despite his irritation and anger, Hatfield had to chuckle. The hellion was smart as a barrel of foxes. Right about here, Hatfield judged he would leave the Old Spanish Trail and strike south. And again he would enjoy a comfortable lead, with his pursuer very much at a loss as to which way he would turn or where he was heading for.

Hatfield tried to take a philosophical view of the matter. Doubtless someone in authority would eventually appear and he would be released. Meanwhile he could only school his soul to patience. He smoked several cigarettes, listening to the chatter of the villagers in the square and when it grew dark he stretched out on the boards and tried to sleep. With scant success due to numerous ambitious fleas and several inquisitive rats that showed a tendency to nibble.

The night seemed endless, but finally morning came, the wan light filtering through the barred window. Two more hours passed and footsteps approached his prison. Bars rattled, the door was opened and a pleasantly modulated voice said,

"*Senor,* come forth."

Hatfield walked out, blinking in the bright sunshine, and faced an immaculately garbed, good-humored, elderly man who regarded him with a questioning and somewhat quizzical eye.

"I fear," said the newcomer, "that my children have been gullible and impulsive. Doubtless, *Senor,* you will have no trouble giving a satisfactory account of yourself. I am Luiz Alvarez, the mayor of this village."

Without speaking, Hatfield drew forth his Ranger badge and showed it to the mayor. Alvarez nodded his head and did not appear overly surprised.

"I suspected some such thing when the word was brought me this morning that my children had captured a notorious robber upon whose head was a large reward. My experience has been that notorious robbers are not so easily captured, whereas an honest man expecting no evil may readily walk into a trap.

"It seems that yesterday evening a man rode into the pueblo on a nearly exhausted horse. He told an excited tale about being pursued by a dangerous *ladrone* who wished to rob him. He spoke *Espanola* like a native of *Mejico* and my stupid children believed he was a kinsman from the south. He bought a fresh horse, paying for it in gold, and rode on, saying that he feared for his life if his terrible pursuer caught up with him. My children armed themselves and lay in wait for the robber."

"And they did it darned efficiently," Hatfield replied with a smile.

"I trust you will not be too angry with them," pleaded the mayor. "They are ignorant and impulsive and were duped by that smooth-talking stranger."

"He duped a lot smarter folks than they," Hatfield returned grimly. "Nope, I don't hold it against them. They thought they were doing the right thing."

"I am gratified," said Alvarez. "And, *Senor*, I trust I can prevail on you to accept my hospitality. My ranchhouse is but a short ride distant."

"Well, I could stand some breakfast and

I sure would like a bath," Hatfield smiled in reply.

Goldy was brought around by an abjectly apologetic *peon*. He appeared to have fared much better than his master. The mayor's horse was hitched nearby. They mounted and headed for the big ranchhouse.

"And that yellow-haired stranger, you are pursuing him?" remarked Alvarez.

"That's right," Hatfield admitted.

"I fear he has escaped you," said the mayor. "I learned that he crossed the river into *Mejico*."

Hatfield nodded, but did not discuss the matter further.

Alvarez's hospitality was lavish and after a luxurious bath, an excellent breakfast and a few hours of needed rest, Hatfield said goodbye to his kindly host and rode off feeling much better physically, at least.

He paused at the village to ask some questions of the humbled *peons* who answered readily.

"South he rode," they said. "South toward the Great River. Four miles to the east there is a ford where doubtless he crossed. And from the ford a trail runs southward through the mountains, a trail much used by the smugglers in the old days, and by the *Indios*. Where does it lead to? Who knows, *Capitan!* Perhaps to where the river of time runs over the edge of the world and is lost in the nothingness beyond. It is a very old trail."

Hatfield thanked the villagers and rode on, south by east till he reached the stately River of the Palms. He pulled up at the ford and sat gazing across the shallow yellow flood. High, many-colored and hazy, the mountains bulked in a serrated mass on the horizon. Blue, purple and red, their misty appearance due to an atmospheric haze caused them to apparently change shape from time to time. Hatfield knew the Apaches called them the ghost mountains, and they looked a fit habitation for disembodied spirits.

It was a vast land there across the yellow river, a land of great distances, where a man might ride for days and never see a human habitation. Mountain, desert, rolling rangeland! The state of Chihuahua alone was almost as large as Texas. And somewhere in all that vastness was the man he sought. To try to ferret him out appeared a hopeless task; but Hatfield had a clue upon which he based his hopes.

Down there he would have no Ranger

authority, and couldn't get any. His only authority would be that which he packed on his hips.

"Well, Caesar crossed the Rubicon and did pretty well afterward," he mused aloud. "So I reckon I can cross the Rio Grande."

He drew forth his Range badge, gazed at it a moment and tossed it into the bushes. He hitched his gun belts a little higher about his sinewy waist, spoke to Goldy and the sorrel's hoofs splashed in the muddy water.

From now on it would be man to man!

19

From village to village in Mexico a story spread, a story that in time grew to be a legend. The story of a tall man with level green eyes who rode a magnificent golden horse and always asked a single question —

"Where is *Valle de las Estrellas?*"

And always the answer was the same,

"*Senor,* we do not know. Of such a place we have never heard. It must be far to the south."

The story spread and spread as the man on the golden horse appeared in village after village. Sometimes he passed on immediately, sometimes he lingered for a while, to rest or to minister to those he might help.

"A strange man," said the villagers. "A strange man and a gallant man, undoubtedly an *hidalgo* of the blood. Kindly, considerate, courteous, causing one to consider him an honored guest. A man good to greet and hard to say farewell to. Always when he departed it was with the words that speed on his way the well-loved traveler: — *Vaya usted con Dios* — Go you with God!

"He was much skilled in what is needful to heal the sick and mend the injured, and he was always ready to give of his skill. And the words he spoke were words of wisdom. Will he come this way again? Who knows. We hope that he will. He was a strange man."

Back and forth across the great state of Chihuahua, Jim Hatfield rode, working south by west on a seemingly endless quest. Robert Morales appeared to have vanished into the mists, and Starlight Valley with the mirages of the desert. Time and again he told himself that it was ridiculous to hope to find a man in this boundless maze where news traveled slowly and a person might live a lifetime in an isolated village without ever meeting his neighbors of the nearest settlement. And there were valleys by the thousand, unknown and unheard of beyond their immediate environment.

But with the dogged persistence of the Rangers he refused to give up the search. He would hear a vague rumor of a place that might be what he sought, ride a hundred miles and when he got there, nothing. Finally he passed beyond Chihuahua and into Sinaloa, the mountain state, wilder and more rugged than anything to the north, but famed for wondrous grazing land in the sheltered valleys. Hillocks grew into hills, and hills into mountains, each range overlying its neighbor, until they soared up in a giant chain raising its spotless and untrodden peaks white and dazzling against the sky.

Sometimes Hatfield rode through gloomy defiles with mountain torrents dashing and foaming against their rocky sides, where the brown, gnarled cliffs shot up to a far-off winding blue slit that was the sky.

At other times, along narrow and rocky paths where often he had to dismount and lead his horse while under his very elbow he could see the white streak that marked the course of a stream that flowed a thousand feet below. It was a land of bare rock and rushing water, a country of the panther, the wolf and the bear. A primitive land where written law was unknown and men lived by a stern code born of necessity.

But some subtle sixth sense, unexplainable but very real, kept telling him that he was nearing the end of his quest. With renewed hope he pushed on through the dreary and inhospitable region.

One night he stayed at the cabin of an old Yaqui-Mexican who lived alone on a fertile mesa and tended his flocks of sheep and goats.

"Valle de las Estrellas?" said his host as they smoked by the fire after the evening meal. *"Si, Senor,* I know. Ride on a score of miles and yet another score and you will come to where the mountains fall away and a wide valley lies between the hills with rich green land and streams that coil like silver snakes in the sunshine. It is well named, for at night the stars seem to brush the mountain tops and fill the valley with their light. There are fine ranches there, particularly that of old *Don* Felipe Gonzales who was the first settler in Starlight Valley. But *Don* Felipe's grandchildren prefer life in the great cities to the south and *Rancho la Paz* has been for sale these many years. Is still for sale, no doubt, for buyers here are few. There is a small pueblo in the northern mouth of the valley,

where many of those who work on the ranches live. Friendly people who welcome the stranger. You go there, *Senor?*"

"Yes," Hatfield replied, "I'll head for there in the morning."

As he rode the southward trail, Hatfield pondered on the almost miraculous something that had led him to his goal. Chance? Or something akin to the unerring instinct that guides the tiny hummingbird across the watery wastes of the Caribbean, and the tern from the Antarctic snows to its nesting place on the Arctic tundras half the width of the world away? Robert Morales had sought sanctuary where not even a breath of his past misdeeds could be wafted; but inexorably his past was closing in on him and he would have to face it in the cold shadows of the lonely finality of death. For Hatfield was convinced that here in this never-never country beyond the horizon, he and his enemy would meet.

The sun was well past the zenith when the mountains fell back as if moved by an invisible hand and Hatfield saw, some three thousand feet below where he sat his horse, a great bowl that glowed in the sunshine like a mighty emerald in a setting of jade. In the foreground was a little town, the buildings looking like doll houses from where he sat, and beyond, the grassland rolled to the misty distances.

A scene of beauty and peace. And here Morales planned to buy a place, doubtless the old Gonzales place of which his host of the night before spoke, and settle down. A laudable ambition it appeared, at first glance. But Hatfield knew it boded ill for the dwellers of this quiet valley. Differences of opinion were bound to arise, and Morales would ride roughshod over all opposition. Tranquillity would become turmoil, a turmoil ruled and directed by a ruthless spirit that would sacrifice anything and anybody to its own ends. Robert Morales would never be satisfied to play a subordinate role anywhere, and all his instincts were evil. He would dominate the community, much to its detriment.

"Seems a snake always crawls into Eden," Hatfield mused. "And too seldom a St. Patrick comes along to drive the critter out." He spoke to Goldy and rode down the winding, rocky track that led to the village.

Hatfield entered the settlement very much on the alert. He wondered what kind of a reception he would receive. His mind was quickly set at rest on that score. He hitched his horse at a convenient rack and entered a small, cheerful looking *cantina* already brightly lighted and glanced about.

The proprietor hurried forward to greet him. Patrons smiled and nodded. He was escorted to a table where he ordered a meal. The order was taken by a bright-eyed *Senorita* who appeared to look with favor on this tall, black-haired visitor from the North. The cook accompanied the food from the kitchen to make sure it was prepared to the patron's liking. Undoubtedly the people of Starlight Valley were friendly to strangers.

Before he finished eating, the *cantina* proprietor came over with a free drink, courteously inquired as to his health and expressed the hope that his stay in the valley would be a long one. It was due to be longer than the Ranger anticipated.

Hatfield had no difficulty procuring lodging for himself and quarters for his horse, the proprietor volunteering to attend to all details of these matters. He remained in the *cantina* for some hours, smoking and sipping excellent wine. From time to time a patron would drop around with a friendly greeting and a moment of conversation touching on general matters. He was asked no pointed questions and refrained from asking any on his part, deeming it to be unwise. He had noted that outside was a square which was evidently the gathering place of the inhabitants of the valley. If Morales was really in the vicinity he would undoubtedly gravitate there sooner or later.

Hatfield went to bed shortly after midnight and slept late. He felt he could use a little extra rest. Before retiring he thought the situation over. He had no definite plan of action, feeling that he could serve his cause best by patiently waiting for Morales to put in an appearance, if he was going to appear at all.

The following day he spent loitering about the square, inspecting the small shops and chatting with the friendly inhabitants of the town. He learned that for many years the community had centered around the great *Rancho la Paz*, but later, other cattle raisers had taken up land and the valley had prospered. The Gonzales family had long ago left the scene and *Rancho la Paz* had been in the hands of a major domo who worked the property and transmitted the proceeds to the owners who now lived in Mexico City. There were trails leading southward from the valley by way of which the cattle could reach markets after a long and arduous drive. The isolation of the spot and the scant communication with the outer world prevented further development.

"But we are happy here, *Senor*," said his informant. "We live in peace with sufficient for our needs. What more can one ask?"

"What indeed?" Hatfield agreed. "Too many folks are always asking something more, wearing their lives away trying to get it and unable to enjoy it when they do get it."

Evening came and still no sign of his quarry. That night he put out a tentative feeler in the hope of gaining information. The *cantina* owner had paused at his table for a brief chat.

"An old fellow up the trail a piece, with whom I spent a night, told me that there was a ranch for sale here," Hatfield observed.

"He must have meant *Rancho la Paz*," the owner said. "For many years it has been for sale, but of late, I understand, it has a prospective purchaser, a man who lived here for a time several years ago and worked on *Rancho la Paz*. He departed and none knew where he went. But a short time ago, he returned, and I understand that he negotiated for the purchase of the property. Doubtless even now arrangements are being made with the owners in Mexico City, which is far from here. Perhaps it will be good for the valley if he succeeds, for the ranch has not prospered as it should in recent years. He who seeks to be the new owner appears to be an able man. He comes here often."

Hatfield nodded and did not pursue the subject. He had learned all he needed to know. For he was convinced that Robert Morales had returned to Starlight Valley with the express purpose of investing his ill-gotten gains in the property he told Mary Morales he wished to acquire.

The evening passed without event and Hatfield went to bed and slept soundly. Morning found him back in the *cantina*. He took a table where he had a view of the trail leading up from the south. He had a premonition that today Robert Morales would come to town.

Shortly after noon he saw a man riding toward the village. He watched eagerly as the horseman grew larger. When he turned into the square, the sunlight glinted on his golden hair. Hatfield rose to his feet, hitching his gun belts a little higher, and walked to the door. He stepped out, his hands hanging loosely by his sides, and paused.

Robert Morales, coming across the square, halted, staring as if he looked upon a ghost. People in the square, sensing drama, drew nearer the silent pair, eyes questioning.

Hatfield spoke, his voice low but clear. "Morales," he said, "it's trail's end. Trail's end and showdown."

Something like a shadow of fear filmed Morales' glittering eyes but was instantly gone. He wet his lips with his tongue.

"What do you plan to do?" he asked, adding meaningly, "I have friends here."

Hatfield knew he was right. Morales had been accepted by the valley and the inhabitants doubtless considered him one of them. He could kill Morales but very likely he would have to fight his way out of the valley, and he had not the slightest desire to injure any of these simple people who had done no wrong. He made a grim decision.

"Morales," he said, speaking Spanish so all would understand, "I can kill you. I know it and you know it. This time you haven't any hanging lamp behind you to blind me. You haven't a chance; you'll be dead a second after you reach. But I'm not here as a peace officer and I'm going to give you a chance, a fighting chance. I see you have a knife in your boot. I have one about the same length. We'll fight it out with naked steel, handkerchief in the teeth, *man to man!*"

A murmur arose. The crowd pressed closer, eyes glowing, faces eager. What Mexican does not understand, and revel in *El Duello* of the Knife? Where two brave men, the corners of a handkerchief gripped in their teeth to hold them together, fight to the death with flashing blades!

Morales' eyes gleamed. Evidently an experienced knife fighter, the proposition appealed.

"Agreed," he said. He shucked off his gun belt, cast it aside and drew his long knife. Hatfield did likewise, then loosened the handkerchief from around his neck, set one corner between his teeth and passed the other to Morales who gripped it with his jaws. The fight was on!

Around and about, back and forth, whirled the glittering blades, thrusting, slashing, parrying, striking sparks as they clashed together, their polished surface flinging back the sunlight in blinding beams.

No man can hope to come scathless from *El Duello* of the Knife. One must take punishment to find an opening for the death stroke. Almost instantly both men were streaming blood from superficial wounds. Morales' knife slashed the top of Hatfield's shoulder. Hatfield's answering stroke laid Morales' cheek open from brow to jaw. Morales' savage returning lunge ripped through the muscles of Hatfield's neck, but not quite deep enough to be fatal. A clashing parry and both men scored again, and the blood spurted afresh.

The watchers crowded closer, groaning, panting, breath catching with each parry, exhaling with a hiss as the long blades drove home. Bets were made, sides were taken, encouragement was called to respective champions. Here were two masters of the knife, two deadly enemies who would fight for as long as a drop of blood remained in their veins. The excitement rose to fever pitch.

Panting, gasping, weakening from loss of blood, the two men fought on, slashing each other's flesh to ribbons, seeking for the one opening that would bring the bloody battle to a close. Morales launched a savage thrust at Hatfield's face. The Ranger threw up his left arm to deflect the blow and the knife plunged through the flexor muscle, the point standing out beyond his shirt sleeve. Morales tugged frantically to free it, but the blade was wedged between the arm bones. He reeled, for an instant off balance.

Hatfield's knife lashed out in a slashing sideways stroke. Morales gave an awful bubbling cry and staggered back. For an instant he stood erect, the blood spouting in fountains from the severed arteries of his throat. Then he crashed to the ground, quivered and was still. A hoarse cheer went up from the crowd.

Hatfield took a slow step forward, gazing down at Morales, and fell so that the two bodies formed a great cross in the dust.

The kindly Mexicans, who love a brave man, withdrew the knife from his arm, stanched the flow of blood and treated his many wounds with their crude but efficient surgery. Though many shook their heads and said that he must die, with ceaseless care and patience they nursed him back to health.

A month after that fatal night in the square, Jim Hatfield sat in front of the cabin that had sheltered him during his slow recovery and talked with his kindly host, the *cantina* owner. To satisfy the

Mexican's curiosity he related the long story of the pursuit of Robert Morales.

"He was bad, but he didn't lack courage," Hatfield concluded.

"*Si,*" nodded the other. "An evil man. I do not think he would have brought happiness here. I knew him when he worked for *Rancho la Paz,* some years ago. I did not like him, although many thought well of him. They believed he was a native of *Mejico,* but I did not. He spoke our language, yes, but not as we of *Mejico* speak it. You yourself, *Capitan,* speak the *Espanola* well, exceedingly well, but I knew at once that it was not your native tongue. You speak it *too* well."

"You're right about that," Hatfield agreed with a laugh. "I'm always trying for the exact word or phrase, which I would never do when speaking English."

"No, I do not believe that man would have brought good to our valley," the Mexican repeated. "All things ended well. *Capitan* will pardon me the moment, *si?*"

He entered the cabin to return a moment later with a thick packet of money.

"Here is much *dinero, Capitan,*" he said. "It was in a belt the man you slew wore beneath his shirt. Take it, *Capitan.* With it *you* can buy *Rancho la Paz.* It would please all greatly to have *you* remain with us."

Hatfield smiled and shook his head. "You keep it," he said. "It is practically impossible to get it back to its rightful owners. Keep it, and use it to help those who need help. That way it'll do some good."

He paused, gazing toward the starry northern rim of the valley. He was thinking of the piquant little face and the blue eyes of Mary Morales.

"Tomorrow I ride north," he said. "I think there is somebody waiting for me up there."

The romantic Mexican smiled his understanding and approval.

"It is well," he said. "Follow to where one's heart's desire leads and one cannot go wrong. *Vaya usted con Dios!*"

We hope you have enjoyed this Large Print Edition. Other Thorndike, Wheeler or Chivers Press Large Print books are available at your library or directly from the publishers.

For more information about current and upcoming titles, please call or write, without obligation, to:

Publisher
Thorndike Press
295 Kennedy Memorial Drive
Waterville, ME   04901
Tel. (800) 223-1244

Or visit our Web site at:
www.gale.com/thorndike
www.gale.com/wheeler

OR

Chivers Large Print
published by BBC Audiobooks Ltd
St James House, The Square
Lower Bristol Road
Bath BA2 3SB
England
Tel. +44(0) 800 136919
email: bbcaudiobooks@bbc.co.uk
www.bbcaudiobooks.co.uk

All our Large Print titles are designed for easy reading, and all our books are made to last.